Happy Birthday, Mia.
Lots of love,
Nana and Papa

Horse in the Mirror

Book One in the Garland House trilogy.

See also *Horse in the Portrait* (Book Two)

and *Horse in the Diary* (Book Three)

Horse in the Mirror

A Garland House Mystery

JENNY HUGHES

BREAKAWAY BOOKS
HALCOTTSVILLE, NEW YORK
2014

ISBN: 978-1-62124-012-9
Library of Congress Control Number: 2014947730

Published by Breakaway Books
P.O. Box 24
Halcottsville, NY 12438
www.breakawaybooks.com

NOTE: For this edition, we have Americanized the spellings (for instance, *color* instead of *colour*) but kept the original British vocabulary and usage. So, for anyone not familiar with some of these terms, here is a brief list with the American equivalents: gorse = a wild shrub common in open land; cheeky = mischievous or impudent; yard = horse barn; loose box = box stall; head collar = halter; bloke = guy; school = riding ring or arena; moors or moorland = a large tract of uncultivated open land; mate = friend; torch = flashlight; Aga = stove; worktop = counter.

10 9 8 7 6 5 4 3 2 1

Chapter One

I leaned forward, keeping low against Aslan's neck, and peered cautiously through the undergrowth. I could see the gray horse and his rider guarding what appeared to be my only route out, patrolling back and forth in the forest clearing. There was only one other chance, a faint, overgrown path seemingly blocked at the end by a solid-looking pile of logs. Aslan moved silently through the tangle of bracken; keeping my body folded low along the powerful line of his shoulders, I let my lower legs touch his sides. He responded instantly, flowing into a buoyant canter, and we surged onward, rapidly approaching the dark mass of the log pile.

Then he was soaring, a big, athletic leap that took us sailing over the topmost log to land, cantering easily, on the other side. We raced flat-out across the springy forest floor, hearing the outraged cry from the other rider as the gray horse turned clumsily and tried to head us off. They stood no chance. Aslan and I reached the safety of the big oak tree and I slowed him immediately, turning in my saddle to laugh and jeer triumphantly.

I really enjoy this game—it's the one where you choose a "home," like a rock or a tree or whatever, and one person has to guard it. The others (or just one other—me—in this case) then go off to hide with the object of reaching "home" before the guard spots them and reaches it first. It's only hide-and-seek, really, and most people stop playing it when they get to age seven, but my friend Tara and I just love this horseback version and play it all the time. My pony, Aslan, is brilliant at winning, but this time I ended up feeling more silly than victorious. The trouble was I hadn't noticed we had an audience—two riders who'd arrived at the clearing by another path and were sitting there, watching us.

"Great jump!" The voice was deep and I looked into the dark eyes of someone who was drop-dead gorgeous and grinning at me with undoubted amusement.

"Oh thanks." I felt very childish and silly. "It's a bit higher than we usually attempt but we were—we were—"

"Playing a stupid game." Tara panted up on her gray pony. "Podge doesn't stand a chance of outrunning Aslan so we tried to outwit them by staying at the only point I thought was passable. I didn't think Ellie would come crashing out of the trees on a path that was blocked off, did I?"

"It took us by surprise too." A slightly younger version of the dark-eyed one grinned at us cheerfully. "I thought we'd jumped everything it was possible to jump in this wood, but we haven't tried that one!"

"And I for one won't." My friend patted Podge and grinned back at him. "I'm Tara, nice to meet you."

"Ricky," the younger one said. "And this is my brother, Jonah."

Jonah and I smiled at each other and I really, really wished I'd been doing something a bit less childish the first time he'd clapped eyes on me.

"This is my best friend, Ellie, who appears to have lost the power of speech," Tara went on. "Which is unusual, as you'll probably find out."

"You're new here?" Jonah asked while I checked out the gleaming lines of the black horse he was riding.

"Mm," I nodded, still feeling definitely poleaxed.

"My godparents bought Critchell Farm last year and invited Ellie and me for the summer," Tara said, chatting away quite easily as if Jonah were just someone ordinary. "This is our third ride out and we're still kind of exploring."

"Have you found the bridle path that leads up to the moor?" Ricky guided his light bay pony to ride alongside Tara and Podge.

"Don't think so."

"We'll show you if you like." Ricky was being very friendly, but I wasn't sure if his brother felt the same.

"Only if you've got time," I said hastily.

"We'll make time," Jonah said very casually, but he looked at me as he spoke and I felt a distinct tremor, like a small ecstatic mouse, run down my spine.

The black horse moved smoothly alongside Aslan. I took a deep breath and tried to act normally.

"Lovely horse," I said. "What's his name?"

"Pharaoh." He grinned suddenly. "Almost as posh as

Aslan, isn't it?"

"Almost." I laughed with him. "Aslan's named after the lion in a book because with his deep chestnut coat and light blond mane he sort of looks like one."

"S'pose he does. He's very striking, especially when he's soaring through the air like just now." He smiled again.

All four horses were walking, very sedately, along the main track of the wood, a broad, sandy path between two banks of solid trees and undergrowth.

"We'd better get a move on." Jonah looked at his watch. "Okay if we canter for a bit?"

Tara and Ricky, who were yakking away as if they'd known each other for ages, nodded, and we all took off into a smart working trot. Aslan is very competitive and loves to race so I knew I'd have to hold on tight to him when we flowed easily into canter. My gorgeous pony spends most of his time at home surging effortlessly in front of Podge, who's very willing and amenable but has no more natural speed than a gerbil. Today was different, though, with the long black legs of Pharaoh eating up the track beneath us. Aslan, pulling like an express train, thundered just behind him, stretching his neck and lengthening his stride in an effort to overtake. My poor arms were beginning to feel like soggy string, and I was quite relieved when Jonah started slowing the pace. We'd arrived at the edge of the wood, a rough, stony path that led back toward Critchell Farm, our holiday home. Jonah, though, led us off the track, opening a gate and walking quietly along the edge of a field. Ricky, bringing up the rear, turned his pony, Tolly, and closed the gate carefully before following us along the length of the field that sloped gently upward. At the top we rode through another gate into a small, pretty copse. It was cool under its canopy of trees; sunlight glinted briefly on our horses' coats as we traveled through the dappled shade.

The trees thinned and cleared and I blinked in surprise as we emerged into the bright, clear air. Spread before us in all its undulating glory was a great tract of moorland, soft greens and browns dotted with vibrant gold splashes of gorse and drifts of purply-pink heather. Pharaoh obviously knew where he was, lifting his head and snorting softly through his nostrils with excitement. Aslan picked up his mood and began to prance, almost rocking backward and forward as he plunged and pulled.

"Okay?" Jonah's warm, dark eyes looked into mine.

"Okay," I breathed and we were off, cantering then galloping across the wide, beautiful moor with the soft wind in our faces. Jonah kept Pharaoh in check, matching the black horse's stride to Aslan's shorter one. It was the most wonderful feeling galloping alongside him, hearing the strong four-time beat of hooves as we flew, simply flew, across the turf. Poised as I was, over the center of gravity with my weight forward and off the saddle, I was really glad both my pony and I were super fit. Even so, I was starting to tire and was happy to see Jonah sit back and give the half-halt aids on his reins. We dropped smoothly into canter, taking the downward transition into walk and then to halt, giving our horses a long rein so they could stretch their necks and relax.

"That—that was brilliant." I'd been going to say *magical* but I thought it sounded a bit soft and girlie. "I can feel Aslan's sides heaving. He's never galloped so far before."

"Really? Sorry, is he all right?" Jonah looked with concern at my pony. I just watched him dreamily.

"He's fine." I pulled myself together firmly. "It's good for him to have a real pipe-opener like that. I want to keep him fit—I start jumping lessons with him when we go home."

"Lessons?" He raised his dark eyebrows. "From what I saw earlier, you two know exactly what you're doing already."

"Thanks." I tried hard not to blush, but it was amazing having Jonah looking at me with such admiration. "I think Aslan's a complete natural but I don't have the control needed to take him round a show ring and that's what I'd really like to do."

"Hiyah." Ricky had come bowling up on Tolly. "If you're talking show jumping, Ellie, you're with the right guy. My brother's great at it and since he got Pharaoh he's just about unbeatable."

"Having a fabulous horse is a pretty big help." Jonah leaned forward and patted the gleaming black shoulder affectionately.

"In that case I'm definitely on to a winner." I leaned forward and hugged my beautiful pony round the neck. "Aslan's the most fabulous horse in the world."

"She's nuts about him," Tara confirmed as she finally pottered up to join us. "They've got all sorts of party tricks. Ellie does impressions, you know, and when she quacks like a duck Aslan cocks his head to one side and looks really puzzled."

"Sounds batty!" Ricky laughed. "Go on, Ellie, give us a demonstration."

I can be quite shy with people I don't know well but today, filled with exhilaration after galloping with Jonah, I hopped out of the saddle and stood in front of my pony.

"Qua-a-a-ack qua-a-a-ack," I said solemnly. Aslan immediately tipped his intelligent head to one side and stared at me intently.

Both Jonah and Ricky laughed uproariously.

"We have a dog who does that to some TV jingles," Ricky said. "But I've never seen a horse do it."

"Maybe that's because not many horses have owners who do duck impressions for them." Jonah grinned at me and I grinned back, feeling a great wave of happiness roll over me as I hopped back into the saddle.

We were walking the horses now, at a nice cooling-down pace, following a curved track through the center of the moor. Jonah rode beside me, pointing out landmarks. Feeling completely at ease with him, I chatted away in a more-than-usual upbeat manner. The route we'd taken was almost a perfect circle, and we were soon returning towards the stony track leading to Critchell Farm. As we crested the last hill Jonah reined Pharaoh in and looked down at the countryside spread out below us.

"There's your farm." He pointed, bending his head to mine.

He was so close I could feel his warm breath on my cheek. I sat very, very still.

"And there—" His finger moved a little westward. "That's where we live. It's called Garland House."

"Wow!" I said. "It's massive, nearly a castle. What do your mates from school think of it?"

"They've never been." He hesitated. "We don't have—er—visitors."

I wanted to ask why not, I'd have had all my friends

there all the time, but his face had gone shuttered and remote so, feeling a bit puzzled, I kept quiet.

"It's only your average Country Manor House," Ricky said cheerfully, bringing Tolly in beside us. "Pretty ordinary really."

"Yeah, right." Tara pushed Podge in between us all and stared down at the lovely old house below. "I live with my mum and my sister in a bungalow, which is what I'd call really ordinary."

I stayed quiet, feeling suddenly deflated. Jonah had moved back, only, I think, to let Tara get a better view, but I was worrying it was because somehow I'd said the wrong thing. As soon as I'd mentioned him inviting anyone to his house he'd seemed to draw away from me, and the lovely feeling of connection between us was now broken. Had I unintentionally stumbled on some dark secret of life at Garland House?

Chapter Two

I didn't say any of this, obviously, just stayed quiet and a bit broody. I didn't think anyone noticed—Tara and Ricky were making a racket, laughing and joking and talking nonstop. We were riding back through the little copse now and Jonah reined Pharaoh in and waited for me to bring Aslan beside him.

"You okay?" His dark eyes looked anxiously into mine. "You're not worrying about Aslan? He's in great shape, I'm sure the extra-long gallop didn't harm him."

"He's fine." I made myself grin cheerfully, determined not to show I was feeling insecure and shaky. "It's—um—nice of you to be concerned."

"He's a terrific horse, I'd hate to think I'd hurt him." *Great*, I thought dismally. *It's my pony he's impressed with, not me!*

Aloud, I said casually, "No problem, he really enjoyed it."

"I was thinking." He hesitated for a moment, sounding kind of stilted and unnatural. "If you'd like to get a few pointers about show jumping before you both start your lessons, you could always come over to our place. We've got a great schooling ring and a full range of colored jumps."

Honestly, he sounded so weird I immediately assumed he'd thought my casual question about friends visiting was a heavy-handed attempt at wangling my own invite.

Deeply embarrassed, I kept my voice casual, even flippant. "Thanks, Jonah, but it'd be a real bore for you, watching a couple of dumb novices flattening all your lovely fences."

"You wouldn't do that." He turned away and moved Pharaoh in front of me again. "But if you don't want to, don't worry." *Why* I couldn't just say, *Oh yes please, that would be the most excellent thing in the world?* I honestly don't know. I can only think I was worrying too much about the "we don't have visitors" remark.

"Come on, Jonah, we're gonna be late." Ricky trotted Tolly toward us, looking at his watch. "We promised we'd give Dad a hand."

"I know," his brother said crossly. My heart sank, knowing it was me who'd irritated him.

"See you tomorrow then, Tara," Ricky said as he unlatched the gate and took Tolly neatly through it. "Come on, Jonah."

Jonah followed him, turning Pharaoh to the left.

"See you, Ellie." He threw the words over his shoulder and I felt another dismal lurch as I watched him ride away.

Tara and Podge plodded through the gate after me and shut it behind them.

"Wasn't that great?" She beamed at me as we turned in the opposite direction, toward the stony track leading home. "Fabulous riding and Ricky is such a *goof.*"

"Good." I tried to feel happy for her. "And you're seeing him again, then?"

"He asked us both over to his farm." She leaned forward and fiddled around with the bridle. "That's all right with you, isn't it?"

"Oh Tara, I don't know about that."

"Why not?" She stared at me in surprise. "Even though he's a bit quiet for my taste, I thought Jonah was a bit of a hunk. You liked him, didn't you?"

"He's—all right." It just wouldn't be cool to shriek, *He's gorgeous!* "But I can't believe someone like him will want a couple of silly kids around."

"What d'you mean?" Tara was indignant. "He's fifteen, only six months older than you, and Ricky's eight months younger than me. There's no way they're gonna think we're silly kids."

"Yeah, right." I was thinking of the daft game we'd been playing when the brothers turned up. "People like them don't go leaping out on each other in the middle of the woods like we do."

"How d'you know they don't?" She nudged her sedately walking gray pony into trot so she could ride beside me. "They're not a different species you know. Ricky and I got on really great and he said he thought Jonah liked you too. He can be a bit stand-offish apparently, but he seemed OK with you."

"He liked Aslan," I said. "He offered to give me a hand with our show jumping."

"There you go!" Tara grinned. "That probably means he fancies you and it definitely means he wants you to visit Garland House. And that's where I'm meeting Ricky tomorrow, so you'll have to come along."

"Okay." I still wasn't sure. "But don't you go saying all that stuff about us fancying each other. It's just for the show jumping, that's all. He made it clear they don't like having anyone at the house."

"That's just him being moody. Ricky told me Jonah's been fretting about some nephew or other," Tara said vaguely, taking her feet out of the stirrups and lying back in her saddle, her boots dangling comically over Podge's shoulders. "Wake me up when we get home."

"One of these days Podge will shy when you're lying there like that and you'll roll straight off!" It always made me laugh to see the placid gray carry on walking while his rider flopped along his back like an oversized rag doll.

"Podge never shies," Tara said firmly. "He's like me, sees no point in making a big scene about everything."

"I'm glad you're so well suited." I put my leg on Aslan, who was trying to dance round a drain cover.

"So are you and yours," she said in a sleepy voice. "Both brilliant but a bit erratic, with not enough confidence in your own abilities, I'd say."

"Abilities yourself!" I said. "And thanks for making me demonstrate our quack-quack routine, by the way. That probably convinced Jonah I was not only childish but a bit soft in the head too."

"Rubbish, he loved it." Tara yawned. "He could do with lightening up a bit and you're the girl to do it once you get over this stupid 'he doesn't want me at his house and he's too old for me' stuff."

"I don't think he's too old." I patted Aslan for being good about walking over the drain.

"Hah!" Tara raised her head. "It's the house thing that's bugging you! Forget it, he asked you along, didn't he?"

It was all very well saying that, I thought the next morning as I dried my hair in front of our bedroom mirror. Jonah had been so warm and friendly before we saw Garland House but it had all changed when he showed me his home. And I couldn't stop thinking about the way he'd said, "we don't have visitors."

Still, at least my hair was looking good for the trip, freshly washed and falling in a nice shiny curtain around my face. I'm lucky I have the silky blond type that's very manageable, and I knew even after wearing my riding hat again in the morning it would look all right when I shook it out. Not that I'd get a chance; Jonah would probably disappear as soon as the show jumping lesson was over. I felt it was worth making the effort though, just in case. When it was time to go I also put on my cutest T-shirt, together with my favorite black breeches. Tara caught me checking my appearance and whistled loudly.

"Wowee! You look great. Jonah's gonna think it's his birthday!"

"Don't be daft." I twanged my hair hurriedly into an elastic band. "I haven't done anything special."

"No, sure." Tara was dressed in her usual baggy top and battered jeans. "You look just the same as always."

I ignored her and whizzed downstairs to get Aslan ready. One of the great things about this holiday was that our ponies were, literally, just outside the back door of the farmhouse where we were staying. At home we have to cycle four miles or persuade our long-suffering parents to drive us to the yard where we stable Aslan and Podge. Here, though, there were fields and a couple of loose boxes right on the doorstep. It was lovely summer weather so the horses had stayed out all night, contentedly grazing, and all we had to do was bring them in and get tacked up. I hopped onto the big gate and looked across the field to where the two heads were cropping grass, one silvery gray with a slate-colored mane, the other a deep, glowing chestnut set off by that startling luxuriant mane of pale gold.

"Aslan!" I called, quite softly, and his beautiful red-gold head came up at once. "Come on, baby!" I crooned and felt a great whoosh of pleasure as he came toward me, breaking into an eager, buoyant canter on the way.

"You lucky thing," Tara said enviously. "I shall have to plod right across the paddock to get my boy—oh, look at the state of Aslan!"

My horse had slithered to a halt and was dropping his soft, velvety nose into my palm. One side was perfect, all gleaming coat and shining mane, but the other was caked in mud, dust, and grass stains.

"He's rolled!" Tara laughed. "And managed to find the only mud patch in the entire place!"

Aslan whickered and I felt his warm breath on my fingers.

"Never mind, mate." I pulled his ears gently. "As long as you enjoyed it, what's a bit of muck among friends?"

His big dark eyes looked into mine and he tilted his head to one side as he often did when I talked to him.

"He's trying to work out what you're saying." Tara slid off the gate and started walking toward Podge. "Give a few quacks, that'll confuse him!"

I grinned and slipped a head collar over the chestnut pony's ears. Once I'd tied him up in the small stable yard it didn't take long to get rid of the dried-on mud. It was a pleasure to see the sheen on his coat emerge from under all that dust. I finished with a few sweeping strokes through his long mane and tail and went off to get his saddle and bridle. Tara had her pony already tacked up.

"Podge only needed a quick brush," she boasted smugly.

"He wasn't dirty at all."

"That's only because he's too lazy to roll," I pointed out. She laughed again.

It wasn't till we were approaching the stony track where Jonah and Ricky had left us the day before that I bothered to look down at myself. The formerly immaculate breeches had a fine coating of dust and horsehair, and a big lump of mud had stuck to the logo on my trendy T-shirt. *Oh well,* I thought philosophically as I brushed myself down. *Don't suppose Jonah will notice what I'm wearing anyway.*

Soon we were approaching the tall wrought-iron gates of Garland House. I started feeling nervous again as I turned in my saddle to look at Tara.

"Did you—um—find out anything about this place?" I tried to make the question sound casual.

"I did ask Duncan and Mary"—they're her godparents—"about the family but they don't know much about Garland House, haven't met anyone from there yet. Duncan said he'd heard some grumpy old man owned it but he wasn't sure."

"I suppose that will be their grandfather," I said slowly.

"Maybe he's the one who doesn't want people coming to the house."

"Are you still on about that? Even if he is an old grouch we're not coming here to see him—it's Jonah and Ricky who asked us." Feeling nervous was making me gloomy. "Well, you can't convince me Jonah was keen on the idea."

"Then why did he invite you?" Tara was maddeningly logical. "Just relax and enjoy yourself, Ellie. You're so wound up you're making that horse of yours jittery."

It was true: Aslan was fidgeting and prancing, tossing his head around and snatching at his bit.

"Steady, boy." I made my voice very calm and tried to unstiffen my tense shoulders and back.

Aslan immediately settled back into a nice extended walk and we passed through the gates and along a wide, curving drive leading to the house. It was beautiful. Lush green lawns and graceful oak trees lined our way, and the eye traveled naturally to where the fine mellow brick rose gracefully to its gabled and turreted roof. It wasn't actually as big as I'd thought, certainly not in the castle bracket, and I still couldn't think why visitors wouldn't be welcome. Still,

Tara was right, I mustn't let it get to me, so I stayed relaxed in the saddle and Aslan behaved perfectly as we got nearer and nearer the house.

"There's Ricky," Tara said suddenly. I saw the younger brother come running toward us.

"Hiyah." His eyes weren't as soulful or his face as good looking as Jonah's, but he was very friendly and welcoming. "You're both here! That's great."

I thought I detected surprise and immediately plunged into doubt. "Is that all right? I mean—Jonah said I could use your school and . . ."

"Sure. He just got the feeling you weren't keen, told me he didn't think you'd be turning up today."

"Oh," I said, thinking, *He's probably gone out for the day and now I feel really stupid.* "I'll—um—I'll go on back home then, shall I?"

"Don't be so daft." Tara shot me an irritated look. "You know you'd love to try some proper jumps."

"But if Jonah's not here—" I began, then blushed hotly as his tall figure appeared from the side of the house.

"I'm here, just didn't think you'd be." He looked at me

and I wished I weren't bright red, that I didn't have mud and hair all over me, and most of all that I could stop being such an insecure ninny.

"Hello," I said weakly. He grinned, that great warm spark back in his eyes.

"Hello. So, do you want to get Aslan warmed up straightaway or do you want to come in for a coffee before we start training or—"

"Coffee would be good," Tara interrupted. I nodded dumbly.

We put our horses in two empty stables in the lovely old yard adjacent to the house and followed Jonah and Ricky into a small room.

"Boots," Jonah said, kicking off his.

We did the same and padded through to a gorgeous sunlit kitchen that was all gleaming pans and geraniums on the windowsill and a big table in the middle. There were two dogs stretched out blissfully in a pool of sunshine; a large tabby cat washed itself by the stove. A slender woman, with the same dark eyes and smile as Jonah, turned round to greet us. The dogs jumped up and joined her, tails wagging furiously.

Ricky waved a friendly hand around. "This is Mum and the black Labrador is Drummer and the hairy mongrel Sidney. Cat's called Charlie even though she's a girl and Dad's probably out digging potatoes." He paused for a breath. "Meet Tara and Ellie, Mum."

Mrs. Barton looked genuinely pleased to see us and as well as mugs of delicious-smelling coffee she pushed a plate of homemade biscuits toward us and told us to help ourselves.

"So, which one of you is the show jumper?" Her bright eyes looked us over. "Jonah was really impressed, can't ever remember hearing him so enthusiastic before."

Jonah's color deepened and he ran his hand through his hair. I was sorry for him; he was so embarrassed in case I thought the enthusiasm was for me. I'd now decided it was only Aslan he was interested in and I felt very strongly that I should have obeyed my first instinct and simply gone straight back home.

Chapter Three

Luckily, before Jonah got so red he burst into flames, there was an interruption. A tall, thin man came bursting into the kitchen, carrying a box of vegetables and leaving a trail of mud behind him.

"Hi! Morning!" He dumped the box on the table and shook hands vigorously. "I'm Tom Barton, thought I heard you arrive. Here's the stuff you wanted, Sue, except the beans aren't quite ready so I've brought sweet corn."

"Thanks, love." Sue Barton picked up a lovely greeny-gold corncob and sniffed it appreciatively. "You forgot your boots again."

His eyes dropped to the floor and he looked guiltily at the big, earth-covered wellies on his feet.

"Sorry." He walked backward out of the room, stepping with exaggerated care onto the muddy footprints he'd already made.

It looked very funny and Tara and Ricky cracked up immediately. To my relief Jonah was laughing too as he grabbed a broom from a cupboard.

"I'll clean up," I said, really glad Tom's entrance had broken into the embarrassing moment, as I happily took the broom from Jonah and swept the trail of mud neatly across the tiled floor.

"Thank you, Ellie," Sue said. "With a husband like mine around I could give you a full-time job doing that."

"No chance," Ricky said wickedly. "Jonah's got big plans for her—they're off to start this show jumping training in a minute."

"Only if you want to, Jonah," I said, feeling too self-conscious to look him in the eye. Instead I fussed around picking up the pile of dirt.

"Sure, I'm cool with that," he replied, sounding equally disinterested, and as I turned I saw the quick, surprised look his mother gave him.

"I thought you were really keen—" she began, but again Tom Barton made a welcome entrance and interrupted her.

"Any coffee left? I'll just have a quick cup then I'll take you two girls on a tour of my gardens if you like."

"Oh Dad," Ricky said with exasperation. "Not everyone who comes here wants to look at your ecologically friendly, organic, self-sustaining bit of paradise, you know."

"I do," Tara said, probably surprising him. "I'm really into all that."

"You can give Ellie and me a hand in the school instead if you want, Rick," Jonah said.

"Nah. I'll join Tara on her tour. Afterward she wants us to take a ride round the grounds. She's never had a good look at a country estate before."

"Okay." Jonah looked at me briefly. "Ready?"

"Yep." I put my cup in the sink, said thanks very much like a nice polite little girl, and followed him back into the boots' room, wishing I could be as natural and up front as Tara was.

"Sorry about my parents," Jonah said, frowning. "They're not used to—um—people coming round."

That expression again! "They're fine," I said, sounding stiff and uncomfortable just like he did. What did he mean "not used to people"? His parents were lovely, very kind and friendly. So was the yet-to-be-seen grandfather really such an ogre that he frightened everyone away? We walked in silence to the stable yard, where Aslan greeted me with a pleased-sounding whicker.

"I've only been gone ten minutes," I pretended to grumble at him.

"You two get on really well, don't you?" Jonah was looking very closely at Aslan. Again I wondered miserably if my horse was the only reason he'd asked me here.

"Mm. We spend a lot of time together and I talk to him a lot."

"Well, let's see how well the partnership's going to work out in the show ring." I was extremely glad to climb aboard my pony. Once I was up here the conversation would be all training stuff and completely impersonal.

We followed Jonah out of the yard, with me still so wound up that my hands clenched involuntarily. Aslan reacted immediately.

"Steady, Aslan, what's the matter, boy?" Jonah had opened the gate into a nicely fenced sand school. "Why is he dancing and jogging like that, Ellie? Is he worried about coming into the school?"

"No, it's my fault." I made myself relax in the saddle, and the chestnut calmed immediately. "I'm—um—a bit tense, I think."

Slight understatement there, but Jonah didn't comment, merely saying, "You do some flat work to warm up while I sort out the poles."

I nodded and, asking for working walk, I moved Aslan along the long length of the school. We've done quite a lot of basic dressage work so I was confident we would execute the movements, figures, and circles necessary to get us moving in a supple, balanced way.

"Good," Jonah said after ten minutes or so. He walked to the center of the school and watched us carefully. "You're going to start your training over very low jumps with poles placed a couple of meters in front of them. This will teach Aslan where the takeoff point should be. I know you've jumped much higher when you've been out and about but that's mostly down to his natural ability. It's relatively easy to jump a single fence, but you both have to learn the skill of riding a course."Now that I was actually doing something, my confidence had returned.

Jonah was a great teacher, incredibly patient and encouraging. Soon Aslan and I were doing grid work exercises, still over low fences and only in trot, but I could feel how well we were moving together. Jonah changed the grid frequently, sometimes in the shape of a box, then a figure of eight, then back to a straight line. At first Aslan got overexcited when he saw the colored poles but Jonah told me to keep the pace slow and calm and my clever horse was soon popping happily over one jump, then the next, then turning, still beautifully balanced to trot and take the third, fourth, and fifth.

"Well done!" Jonah gave me a brief but spine-tingling smile. "That'll do for today, I think. He enjoyed that a lot and you must always, always end on a high note."

"Right." I was surprised at how tired I felt.

I'd imagined myself belting round the ring leaping huge fences so you'd think the trotting poles and tiny jumps would take nothing out of you. In fact it had meant a lot of concentration and hard work, and my legs and brain felt quite jellified and spongy. Jonah was clearing the poles, stacking them neatly in a corner. I stayed on Aslan's back, wondering if I should offer to help. It sounds so stupid the way this awkward, unnatural scratchiness between us was stopping me doing anything normal. I mean, all I had to do was say, *D'you want a hand?* but now that the lesson was over, all my uncertainty was back.

"Um," I said, which was hardly going to lighten the atmosphere. "Thanks a lot for that. Should I go now or wait for Tara, or what?"

"Whatever you like." He shoved his hands in his pockets and didn't look at me. "If I know Dad and Ricky it'll be ages before she gets back." I still sat there like a stuffed lemon. "Maybe I should go then."

He shrugged and I wanted to yell and scream, *What's your problem? If you didn't want me here you shouldn't have said to come over!* I didn't, of course, and simply turned Aslan, walked him out of the school, and started heading toward the drive. The sun was still shining but there was no brightness in the day for me. Stupid tears prickled behind my eyes and I felt my shoulders and spine sag with disappointment. The lesson had been great, my gorgeous pony had been wonderful, but the warm light that I was sure had been in Jonah's eyes had gone and it seemed he couldn't wait to get rid of me. Filled with self-pity and slumping along like a sack of overripe tomatoes, I wasn't aware of anything around me, so when a black streak, followed by a furiously barking gray-and-white streak, appeared out of nowhere and tore across the path directly in front of us, I was completely unprepared. Aslan must have been half asleep himself. I felt a sudden tremor of shock run through him and he shot sideways, half rearing in fright. I don't fall off often—I've never thought it was much fun—and as I hit the ground I very quickly remembered why. Thank goodness I was still wearing my helmet. There was a loud crack as I landed, which I was told later was the sound of my helmet (luckily not my head) making contact with the ground. I also wasn't aware that Aslan, after his first terrified plunge and frenzied gallop across the lawn, turned and came back to where I lay, completely unconscious, in the middle of the drive. Sue Barton, hot on the heels of the two dogs, saw everything. By the time she reached the scene my horse was standing beside me, lowering his head to nuzzle gently at my outflung arm.

"It was so sweet," she told me later. "I've never seen a pony do anything like that. When we come off ours they just head straight for home without us."

"Ellie and Aslan have a very special relationship." Jonah bent to look at me where I lay on their big, squashy sofa.

"Is he all right?" My first thought was for my horse and my second was a surprised pleasure that the glow was back in those deep, dark eyes.

"He's fine. We've checked him over and made him comfortable in one of the stables."

"Thanks," I said sleepily. "I'd better take him home."

"You stay right where you are." Sue was very firm. "The doctor's on his way to check you over."

"No need." I tried to sit up. "I'm okay."

"Thanks to your hat and no thanks at all to our renegade dogs."

"What—what exactly happened?"

"Tom took Tara and Ricky into the nature reserve," Sue said rapidly. "And the dogs stayed with me because they're not allowed. I opened the back door and Drummer saw a rabbit. He flew straight past, followed by Sidney. Sidney's hopeless; he has no idea why they're both running but he finds it very exciting and barks a lot. The rabbit shot round the house and across the drive just in front of you, and the dogs kept going. Aslan must have been terrified but, bless him, like I say he came straight back."

"He's wonderful." I raised a hand and cautiously felt the back of my head. "Did the dogs catch the rabbit?"

"They never do." Jonah bent his face close to mine. "Are you really sore? We took your helmet off and it's cracked."

"I'll have to get a new one." My fingers probed a fair-sized lump. "Still, that's better than needing a new head."

"Absolutely," Sue said. "Especially when the one you've got is so pretty." She moved across the room to look out the window. "Oh good, here's the doctor's car. I'll let him in."

As she left Jonah straightened up and I wondered drearily if he was going to go all remote again.

"Sorry my mother keeps saying all this embarrassing stuff," he said awkwardly. "Like I told you, we're not used to visitors and she's going a bit over the top."

"It's all right." It would be nice if he thought I was pretty too but I supposed that was too much to wish for.

I was about to have another go at sitting up when Sue and the doctor came in. Jonah gave me one last amazing smile and went out. The doctor pummeled me about, asked me questions, and got me walking (slowly) round the room.

"Keep her quiet for a few days and observe her, and she'll probably be fine, but call if she seems forgetful or has a headache."

"I'll be quiet," I promised, feeling, if I'm honest, slightly fragile. "I'll just ride Aslan back and—"

"No way!" Sue took my arm and led me back to the sofa. "I'll ring Tara's godparents and explain about the fall and that you'll be staying with us till you're fit again."

"There's no need," I began as she carefully tucked a cover over me.

"There's every need. The accident was our fault and I'd never forgive myself if we didn't try to make amends."

I felt too sleepy to argue any further but as I drifted into a doze I remember thinking that it was kind of odd behavior coming from a family who didn't like visitors. What exactly would be the reaction of the rest of them—particularly the crabby old grandfather—when they found out I was staying?

Chapter Four

When I woke up I was even more bemused. The room I was in, a comfortable, homely place, was now full of people. I blinked rapidly, trying to work out if they were all Bartons and if any of them looked old and furious, then realized I knew them all. They were Tara, Ricky, Jonah, Sue, Tom, Duncan, Mary, Drummer, and Sidney. Well, okay, I know the last two are dogs, but they were taking up a lot of space with their tail wagging.

"Ellie! You're awake!" Tara rushed up to me looking all emotional. "We were going to call the doctor again in case the bump on your head was worse than he thought."

"Why would it be?" I yawned and sat up.

"Because you've been sleeping so long." She peered earnestly into my eyes.

"I was tired," I explained reasonably.

She laughed and turned to her godparents. "She was tired!" she said and I wondered if maybe they'd gone deaf.

"You're sure you're all right, Ellie?" Mary sounded really worried, and I immediately felt guilty.

"I'm fine, honest." I pulled the cover aside and swung my feet to the floor. "It was only a bit of a bump."

"Even so you're to do as the doctor said and stay where you are." Sue hurried over and lifted my legs back onto the sofa. "Tell her, Jonah."

He was looking at me. "It'll be easier not to argue," he said, so I sank back and let Sue fuss round covering me up again.

"Sue and Tom want you to stay here at Garland House for a day or two," Mary said, speaking s l o w l y and c l e a r l y as though I'd had the sense knocked out of me. "Is that okay with you?"

"Sure," I said, thinking it was just fab as long as Grandfather wasn't around.

"And I'm staying too," Tara put in.

"Yeah? That's really nice." I was still somewhat worried about the old and furious one, but it would be better if my

44

friend was with me. "Are you sleeping on a sofa too?"

"No, no, there's a room ready for you both. In fact you could have one each but we thought Tara could keep an eye on you through the night."

They'd obviously never seen my friend sleep. She takes about three seconds flat to drift off and you can drop small bombs around her and not wake her up. Still it would be nice to have her around and maybe she could shed some light on this mysterious no-visitors-please-we-have-a-weirdo-granddad thing surrounding the Barton family. Duncan and Mary checked me over and kissed me good-bye several times and promised they'd tell my parents but not worry them.

"Tell them she landed on her head." Tara had regained her usual charming manner, "so no harm done."

"Thanks a lot," I told her. "Actually there is damage—look at my poor helmet!"

"Tom's going into town tomorrow to replace that," Sue said. "Although you won't be wearing it for a day or two."

I pulled a face. "That means no riding."

"Quick, aren't you?" Ricky grinned. "You'll have to wait

a bit for your next jumping lesson. How did it go—Jonah's not said much."

"Good," I said, "it was good."

"We kept the jumps low and built up the sequence, not the height of the fences," Jonah said. "Ellie and Aslan were terrific."

"So where were you going when you fell off?" Tara frowned at me. "You were on the drive, not in the school."

"I thought you'd be ages so I started making my way home," I explained slowly, remembering how miserable I'd felt because Jonah didn't want me around.

"Honestly, Jonah!" Sue said, fixing him with an irritated stare. "Why you had to be so aloof and couldn't ask Ellie to stay, I just don't know. We're all perfectly aware you were dying to spend the day with her!"

"Well, now he gets to spend several days instead," Ricky broke in swiftly as the color suffused poor Jonah's face yet again.

"Let's give these kids some peace." Tom tactfully took his wife's arm and steered her toward the door. "Come on, Duncan, Mary, we've got some good strong coffee on the go in the kitchen."

Jonah had shoved his hands in his pockets and was stared mutely at the floor till they'd gone. "Sorry—"

"Don't you go apologizing for the things Mum says." Ricky gave him a hefty shove. "She doesn't mean to embarrass, she just says it like it is."

I blinked again. Did he mean Jonah actually did want me around? This was definitely something worth getting a bump on the head for.

As if she knew what I was thinking, Tara flung herself down in a chair and grinned at me "Feeling better?"

"Okay," I said guardedly.

It was all very well for everyone else to keep on about how much Jonah and I liked each other, but you can't just come right out and say it. Or at least I can't, and neither, apparently, could Jonah. Still, the glow was definitely back. He seemed perfectly happy that I was going to be around the place for a while and that, at the moment, was good enough.

"How did the tour go?" I decided to change the subject. "I hear you went somewhere called the nature reserve."

"Oh Ellie." Tara's face lit up. "It's fabulous, the whole place is fabulous! Tom's got this amazing walled garden with vegetables and fruit and herbs and everything's natural, no chemicals, and no sprays. He catches all the rainwater in barrels and recycles everything and makes compost and plants things like marigolds next to broad beans to keep off blackflies so it's all productive and beautiful at the same time."

"Lovely," I said, quite amused by her enthusiasm. "Is this the kind of thing your mum wants to do at home?"

"Mm, and Tom's given me loads of ideas for her. One of my favorites is going out at night and picking all the slugs off the plants and then feeding them to the chickens in the morning. Extra protein for the chickens and less holes in the lettuces!"

"You don't actually have chickens," I pointed out, but she ignored me and carried on enthusing about the Bartons' setup for what seemed hours.

"I still don't know about the nature reserve," I reminded her when she took a breath.

"That was Dad's brainchild too," Ricky said proudly.

"He talked the old man into letting him fence off the whole western corner of the grounds. He just cleared any rubbish and cleaned up the pond and then left it virtually undisturbed for several years. Now it's an absolute haven for wildlife of all sorts—that's why Drummer and Sidney aren't allowed inside."

"Wow." As well as being impressed, I was intrigued by the first mention of the man I referred to inside my head as Grumpy Old Grandfather. "Does—does the old man like it too?"

"He—" began Jonah, and then groaned as his mother put her head round the door. "Come and fetch a drink for everyone. Ellie's got a special glucose-and-fruit mix to pep her up."

Jonah went out and I watched Ricky and Tara start a play fight with the dogs, each doing tug-of-war with a couple of rope toys. Drummer was really into it, pretending to growl and tug-tug-tugging with great force so that Tara had a job holding on. Sidney, the mongrel, hadn't a clue, just kept letting Ricky win the rope then barking happily every time he sent it flying across the room.

"Now fetch!" Ricky would say, and the gormless dog stared fixedly into his face as if to say, *Fetch what?*

"Hopeless hound!" The younger Barton plodded across the room for the fifth time and picked up the rope himself. Jonah came in with a tray. "Mum says to keep the noise down. Ellie's an invalid, remember."

"Invalid!" I sat up and put my feet on the floor. "No chance. Let's try this revolting fruit thing then."

It was lovely actually, and although I did feel just slightly wobbly I also felt very happy, completely and utterly different, in fact, from the sulky self-pitying girl who'd gone slouching off toward home an hour or so earlier. The entire Barton family were being so nice to me and it was very pleasant being pampered and fussed over. Tara and I were given a lovely lunch and Sue and Tom just couldn't have been more welcoming or friendly hosts. I was worried they were blaming themselves (or at least their dogs) for my accident and was insistent that it was me, myself, who was mainly to blame.

"I wasn't concentrating," I said. "Just slopping along taking no notice and you can't ride Aslan like that. He's brilliant but he can be spooked very easily."

"Just the opposite of Podge," Tara put in proudly. "You could set off firecrackers under him and he wouldn't turn a hair."

I saw Jonah raise his eyebrows and I smiled, knowing he was thinking he'd rather have the more volatile Aslan any day. He saw me and smiled back. We'd finished lunch and were all sitting round the kitchen table, chatting easily and comfortably. It was obvious the four Bartons were lovely, friendly people, and they all seemed very happy for us to be in Garland House. I didn't like to pry and keep asking the rest of them questions but when they announced they were off to do the animals' midday feeds and other chores, I couldn't wait to grab Tara and start finding out. She, on the other hand, was all agog to know what had gone on between Jonah and me to make me want to go home.

"Did you have a row?" she asked.

I shook my head. "No, I—just thought he didn't want me here."

"Your trouble is you think too much," she said darkly. "It was totally obvious to everyone else that he was dead

51

keen. You heard what Sue said."

"Yeah but I thought she was just being an interfering mother; mine says embarrassing personal stuff like that sometimes too. And it worried me, Jonah's remark about no one coming here. Why don't they?"

"Well, they will now, obviously," Tara said irritatingly. "I mean, everything's changed hasn't it?"

"How? Is it to do with the grandfather?"

She stared at me "What grandfather?"

"Theirs of course." I was finding this hard work. "I presume he's the one who doesn't like visitors."

"Silas you mean?"

"Who's Silas?" I nearly yelled.

"Silas Crawford, the old man who owned Garland House."

"Owned? You mean it doesn't belong to the Bartons?"

"Well, it does now. He died last month and left it to them. Quite right too when you think Sue and Tom looked after him for twenty years."

"D'you mean they worked for him?"

"Yes, that's exactly what I mean." She looked at me

again. "Are you sure that bang on the head hasn't scrambled your brain? You're being very slow about this and it's perfectly straightforward."

"I thought the old man I kept hearing about was Jonah and Ricky's grandfather, and I also thought he was the one who wouldn't have visitors."

"Yeah, he was, only he was Silas, not a grandfather. He bought the house about thirty years ago. He was already a loner, practically a hermit when Sue and Tom came as housekeeper and gardener. Even back then, Tom was fired up with enthusiasm to do something special with the grounds and Sue—well, you you've met her, she just loves looking after people. They were very fond of the old boy. Ricky and Jonah didn't mind him either even though he was a bit of a crank. I s'pose he was like a granddad to them and although Silas didn't like anyone else around he definitely considered the Bartons his family."

"And now they're the owners of Garland House." I thought it a nice story. "That must be great."

"It is, because Tom's keen for people to see the success he's made of the grounds and gardens. He wants to open up the place to eco-tourists who want to stay on an organic farm and learn how it's done."

"It must be nice for them being able to invite people here." I thought about it. "No wonder Jonah sounded a bit weird about asking me. I bet we're the first friends who've ever been here."

"Yeah, we are, and I'm glad you two have finally worked out you both like each other!"

"Okay, okay, so maybe I'm a bit slow compared with you! I feel a lot happier about staying now I know there's no grumpy old granddad to jump out at me."

"I'd like a look round the rest of the house, wouldn't you? They should be back soon—how long does it take to feed goats and chickens and ducks?"

"What sort of question is that? Ooh, what about Aslan? I ought to give him a feed."

"You're all right, he's had one, and we've turned him and Podge out in the field next to Pharaoh and Tolly. First thing your boy did was have another roll."

"He deserves it, coming back like that to check if I was all right."

"Yeah, right, though some would say he'd have done better not dumping you on the ground in the first place." Tara doesn't always seem to appreciate Aslan's finer points.

I noticed her looking at her watch and said quickly, "You can go out and give the Bartons a hand if you want. I'll stay here like a good girl."

"Sue wants someone to be with you all the time in case you take a turn for the worse." She looked at me dispassionately. "Though how we're s'posed to tell, God knows."

"Thanks!" I said and thumped her with a cushion.

She went to grab another one to retaliate but stopped herself. "Better not hit you back today. I'll save it up for when you're better."

I thought it was funny being treated like this fragile little invalid but hoped it wouldn't go on too long. Being cooped up indoors isn't my idea of fun and I knew I'd soon start missing riding my beloved Aslan. Still, for a day or so, there were worse things than being mollycoddled in a nice, interesting house like this—and the thought that Jonah was genuinely pleased I was there was one great big fat bonus!

Chapter Five

The rest of the day passed by in a pleasant kind of blur. Everyone was very kind and attentive, and it wasn't until I looked in a mirror and saw how pale I was that I understood why. Like I said, I don't fall off my horse too often and it had shaken me up more than I realized. Despite the morning nap I'd had I was still a bit sleepy and went to bed at a ridiculously early hour. Tara, bless her, accompanied me upstairs, yawning theatrically and saying she was tired too, but I knew she was really doing her keeping-an-eye-on-Ellie thing. Our bedroom was nice, with pale walls and bright curtains and comfortable twin beds.

"This house is much more ordinary than I thought," I said to Tara.

She grinned wickedly. "What were you expecting—something gothic and creepy with long dark corridors and suits of armor everywhere?"

"Something like that." I looked around "But it's practically the same as our house only bigger."

"That's because this side is relatively modern, Ricky told me. The western end is original and that dates back hundreds of years apparently. We can have a good look round tomorrow if you're feeling better."

"I'm fine," I said, clambering thankfully into bed, where, would you believe, I put my head on the pillow and immediately fell asleep for over ten hours.

I'd probably have gone on snoozing till lunchtime if Tara hadn't drawn back the curtains and let in a flood of early-morning sunshine.

"Morning." She came over and peered closely into my face.

"Stop it," I said ungratefully. "What d'you think you're doing?"

"Checking that you're all right." She moved back and regarded me solemnly, tilting her head to one side so she reminded me of Aslan. "You're a more normal color at least."

"Cheeky cat." I got out of bed and wandered over to

the window. "Lovely day—oh look, you can see our ponies!"

Aslan was lying down, completely flat out, and probably blissfully snoring while Podge stood quietly next to him.

"My horse is doing the same as me," Tara said. "Keeping guard over his friend."

"I don't need guarding." I'd had enough of all this attention. "Come on, let's go out and see them."

Although it was only about six o'clock (I told you we'd gone to bed really early!), the Barton family were already up and doing their stuff.

"We have breakfast about seven, once the morning feeds are done." Sue was stirring a big pot of something on the stove. I must have wrinkled my nose because she laughed and said, "Don't worry, this is for the hens, not for you. I was going to give you breakfast in bed."

"No way." I felt embarrassed again. "I'm absolutely fine, honestly."

"You look better." She gave me the same once-over Tara had. "But you still have to take it easy."

"I promise," I said. "We're going over to see Aslan and Podge. D'you want anything doing while we're out?"

"On your way back you can collect the goats' milk, please. Tom will have finished milking by then." Tugging on our boots, we left the house and started walking across the grass of the nearby paddock.

The sun was already warm, giving the drops of dew that clung to every green blade a diamond-bright glitter. I breathed in the soft morning air and thought there couldn't be a more beautiful start to a day. I didn't call Aslan, just moved quietly toward him, admiring the way the clear light gleamed on the deep chestnut of his coat. As we approached, Podge whickered softly and Aslan raised his head immediately.

"Good morning, you lazy lump," I said affectionately. He blew happily down his nose in return.

I knelt beside him, put my arms round his neck, and kissed him very soppily. It's absolutely lovely when your horse trusts you enough to allow a cuddle while he's lying down. In nature their main defense is flight so they must feel very vulnerable in that position. Aslan, though, was quite happy to stay there while I lay down between his hooves, resting my head on his belly. He turned to look at me, curving his neck right over me as though he was giving me a cuddle too. One of the tricks we can do is to spread a blanket nearby when we're doing this. I then say "Aslan, I'm cold," and he picks a corner up in his teeth and pulls the blanket right over us. If I put on a baseball cap he's also learned to grab the peak and whip it off my head, tossing it through the air as if he hates me wearing it.

None of these things is particularly useful, but they all amuse my friends and me and they demonstrate the complete trust Aslan has in me. It's a lovely, lovely feeling and as usual I thoroughly enjoyed that morning's contact with my adored pony. I gave him one of Tom's organic carrots and one last pat.

"You're having a couple of days off," I told him. "So don't go getting all flighty and wound up with all that surplus energy."

"Jonah said he'd give Aslan a lesson on the lunge." Tara had finished checking Podge's hooves. "So he won't be too fizzy when you start riding again."

"I'll enjoy watching that." I started heading back for the gate. "I've tried it a couple of times myself but I kept getting tangled up."

We collected the goats' milk as requested, helped Ricky round up a couple of chickens who'd strayed into the vegetable garden, and then went back to the kitchen. Jonah was the last to appear, and when he came in his eyes went straight to me.

"You look great," he said. "Um—I mean much better."

I preferred great, but I was beginning to figure him out.

"Can we have a guided tour of the house today?" Tara asked when we were putting the breakfast dishes in the dishwasher. "I could stay out there in the grounds forever, but if Ellie's got to be kept quiet a look round indoors would be ideal."

A quick glance flashed between Tom and Sue. Sue sighed. "Twenty years of Silas never allowing anyone here means we find the thought of showing anyone around quite strange, but we'll have to get used to it."

"Oh don't worry, I'll find something else to do—" I put in quickly.

"Not it's fine, it'll be a pleasure." Sue leaned over and checked a calendar hung on the kitchen wall. "Oh, we can't this morning—we're meeting the owners of a couple of shops to discuss them taking some of our produce."

"Ricky and I will do the showing round," Jonah said, looking at me. "If that's okay? I mean, we're not as good at the history of the place but—"

"That's fine," Tara said. "As long as there's something spooky you can tell Ellie. She imagined the place to be a lot more creepy."

"I'm sure the boys will do their best," Tom laughed. "Though unfortunately we don't know much about Garland's early days."

"And we've never seen any ghosts." Ricky waved his arms above his head and made spectral noises. "But we can invent some if you like."

"Oh no, you're not going to leap out at Ellie covered in a dust sheet or something," Sue said firmly. "We promised Duncan and Mary we'd look after her, not frighten her to death."

"Honestly, I'm perfectly all right." I was getting really

fed up with all this fuss. "You can hardly feel the bump on my head now, and I feel fine."

"Even so . . ." Sue followed Tom out of the kitchen. "Behave yourselves, you lot."

"Right then, ladies and gentlemen," Ricky said. "Form an orderly queue and we'll commence the official tour of Garland House. Feel free to ask questions at any point though an accurate answer is not necessarily guaranteed."

"Dope!" Jonah gave him a friendly shove and grinned at me. We followed Ricky into a very traditional hallway with a black-and-white tiled floor and paneled walls.

"Bedrooms and bathrooms up there." Ricky waved a hand at the wide staircase. "But they're all pretty much the same and you've slept in one so we shan't bother going up."

It was a similar story with the dining room and a small study but then Ricky flung open a door and said in a dramatic, booming voice, "And now—the original, the ancient, the real Garland House. Dan-dan-dan!"

"Shut up, you." Jonah pretended to clout him. "You heard what Mum said. Come on through, Ellie and Tara, and take no notice of my idiot brother."

We were in another hall, its stone-flagged floor and roughly plastered walls quite different from the first. Even the air felt older, with a slightly musty tinge than you could smell and almost see. The windows were much smaller so the light was dimmed, and it was very, very quiet. We walked across to the staircase, and although we only had socks on our feet the sound echoed eerily. Ricky, seeming quite unaffected, galloped cheerfully up the stairs, pausing to point out an ancient-looking tapestry that took up most of the wall.

"I thought there would be family portraits." I peered at the faded, though still lovely, colors.

"Did you?" Jonah was smiling at me. "Dozens of decayed Bartons peering down at you from the walls?"

"Exactly that." I was feeling so much more comfortable with him now that I didn't mind owning up. "Of course I didn't know about Silas Crawford then."

"Ellie thought the old man she heard about was your grandfather," Tara informed them. "And that he was some kind of people-hating monster."

"Silas was definitely not a monster, but the hating-people bit's about right." Jonah looked at me, almost shyly. "No wonder you were so wary of coming here, Ellie."

"What about when Silas first came here, before your parents came along to look after him? Was he completely and utterly alone?" I was intrigued by the concept of the solitary, hermit-like man.

"He had an old cook and for a few years there was his nephew, Roger, who stayed here when his parents died."Tara looked around the chill, lofty landing. "Not exactly a welcoming place for a kid."

"Rick and I grew up here," Jonah reminded her crossly. "And we love it."

"So you did!" Tara pulled a comic face. "We've never been in a house like this, have we, Ellie? The bit where you live is really nice, but this end's a bit spooky."

We were now being shown some bedrooms that were furnished with heavy, dark oak pieces, dark, musty fabrics, and scuffed flooring.

"If Mum and Dad's plans take off all these will be refurbished and brought up to date. We're hoping that people will come to stay while they learn about self-sufficiency and organic gardening."

"I'm looking forward to that." Ricky stopped to look in a big mirror with a heavy gilt frame. "Look at us lot peering out of the mist like a foursome of ghosties."

He was right: The old glass was spotted and dimmed with age, and our reflections swam hazily in the dim light.

Tara gave a dramatic shudder and said, "I don't think I'd bother coming here till your parents have spiffed it up a bit. What do you use it for anyway? You don't sleep here surely?"

"No, we don't come upstairs often, but we sometimes go in the library that's downstairs."

"Can we go down and see it?" I wanted to get away from the old rooms and thankfully trotted back downstairs.

"Here you go." Ricky opened a door and Tara and I gasped.

It was amazing, a proper floor-to-ceiling library just like you see in old films. It had leather armchairs, Persian rugs, and all four of its walls were lined with row upon row of shelves, each one full to bursting with hundreds and hundreds of books.

"Terrific isn't it?" Jonah was watching my face as I gazed round, trying to take it all in. I reached out and touched a book's leather spine. "Are they all real? I mean can you actually read them?"

He and Ricky burst out laughing. "That's the general idea of a library isn't it—books you can actually read?"

"Who chose them all?" I was looking at some of the titles. "Silas?"

"No, they came with the house. Most of the all stuff did, though it was a bit wasted on Silas. He was never interested in it. I don't know why he bought Garland House in the first place."

"How weird." Tara was gaping around just like me. "My mum would love all this stuff and she'd find out everything she could about the house's history."

"Not Silas, though I expect once the house is in our family we'll do some investigating." Jonah looked quite proud when he said it and I realized how fond he was of the place.

"When is it officially yours?" I thought that as the old man died several weeks ago it would all have happened by now.

"The will goes through something legal called probate," he said. "Which in this case should be pretty quick as it's all so simple. Silas left everything to Mum and Dad, with not even any legacies to Cats' Homes or anything."

"Ooh, is this him?" Tara had pounced on a photo in a leather frame.

"Yeah, though it was taken years ago." Jonah looked at it. "When I was little I never believed it was Silas because by then he wore his hair long and had a real whiskery beard."

"That sounds more like my idea of a recluse or hermit or whatever," I said, having found the photo disappointingly ordinary.

"Hey," Tara said, replacing the frame on a small table. "What about the nephew? The one who came to stay with Silas? Why wasn't he mentioned in the will?"

"He died a while back." Jonah didn't seem to mind all the questions. "Silas hadn't seen him for years."

"Why not? Did they fall out?" I was curious; I love all this family history, feuds and all.

"Sort of, but it was before we were born. Roger was here when Mum and Dad came for their interview, but he inherited some money when he was eighteen and just took off. Apparently he wanted to see the world."

"And did he?" I asked.

"I guess so. He died in America, so he certainly got that far."

"And he had no family?"

Jonah looked at me. "Persistent little thing, aren't you? Are you worried that the wicked Barton family are duping the rightful heir out of his inheritance? You don't have to fret on that score—even though he's not named in the will, my parents have advertised for any news. I don't think they should; why risk some long-lost relative turning up and wanting a share?"

"My brother's a natural worrier, Ellie." Ricky, laid-back as usual, grinned at me. "I keep telling him things like that only happen in books."

I remembered Tara saying Jonah was "fretting about a nephew" and I smiled sympathetically at him. I could certainly understand now why he'd seemed so withdrawn when he'd talked about the house that first day.

"Ellie, over here." Tara was peering out the window. "The library overlooks the nature reserve I told you about, come and look."

I walked over to join her, not suspecting for a moment that I was about to get my first glimpse of something that would prove to have the most amazing effect on the entire future of Garland House.

Chapter Six

To be honest, not knowing that, my first reaction was of disappointment. I hadn't quite known what to expect, but the phrase *nature reserve* had conjured up all sorts of exciting pictures in my mind. I didn't imagine I'd look out and see loads of wild animals prowling around, but I did think there'd be more than just trees and undergrowth. There were birds—even from inside the house you could hear them singing and chattering—and once or twice I noticed the branches of a beech tree dip and sway as a squirrel jumped around in it.

"I can't see anything." I craned my neck, pushing my face against the windowpane.

"That doesn't mean there's nothing there," Tara said, quite irritably. "We saw a vixen taking food back for her cubs and a badger's prints and loads of rabbits—"

"Okay," I said mildly. "Maybe this isn't the best view-point."

"You do need to go in," Jonah agreed. "And even then you don't always see much but it's a nice feeling to know it's all happening around you in a completely natural way. I'll take you for a walk through when you're better."

"I'm better now!" I was fed up with this bump-on-the-head stuff. "But I'd rather ride through if we're allowed."

"Yeah, we take the horses in sometimes, very quietly ob-viously, but not the dogs." Jonah grinned at me. "You've seen Drummer and Sidney in action—they'd be chasing everything that moved, which isn't quite what Dad had in mind when he developed the idea."

"Look, Jonah." Ricky pointed to a gap in the books where three tarnished-looking silver cups stood. "How about we clean those up and use them as trophies for the horse show?"

"Oh yeah." Jonah reached up and lifted one down. "They should shine up pretty well."

"When's the show?" I asked, finding the subject a lot more interesting than invisible squirrels.

"At the beginning of September," Jonah said, polishing the cup with his sleeve. "Any chance you'll still be here?"

"We go home on the fifth," Tara said. "Is the show going to be here at Garland House?"

"Yep," Ricky said proudly. "It's on the third and it's the first ever to be held in the grounds."

"Brilliant!" I really meant it. "We can enter the mounted games competitions, Tara."

"No fear. Podge and I came last in everything at the Pony Club rallies."

"Hey!" Ricky always seemed to yell when a thought struck him. "Why don't you and Aslan go in for the novice jumping class, Ellie? You could win one of these—er—beautiful cups."

"I'd love to." I felt a tremor of excitement at the thought. "But I don't know if we'd be ready."

"You should be." Jonah looked enthusiastic too. "You've both got a lot of talent, but it'll take a good bit of work."

"I'll practice every day," I said eagerly. "If that's all right with you of course?"

"You're kidding aren't you?" Ricky pretended to swoon.

"How do you feel about seeing this girl and her pony that often, bro?"

"I think I could bear it," Jonah said solemnly. I felt that extraordinary tiptoeing sensation down my spine again.

We took the cups with us when we left the library, and I'm pretty sure Tara, like me, was quite glad to be back in the warm, friendly atmosphere of the kitchen. We spread some old newspaper on the table and Jonah, Ricky, and I started work with some silver polish to see if we could get the tarnished cups looking more like trophies. Tara sat with us, making copious notes in a notebook.

"Tips for my mum," she explained. "Our garden can't run to a nature reserve, but we could turn some of the lawn into a vegetable plot."

"Your ma will have to pay us a visit," Ricky said, polishing vigorously. "Dad's dead keen to spread the word."

It was very pleasant sitting in that cheerful room with the dogs and cat dozing contentedly nearby and the big kettle making a soft singing sound from its place on the hot plate of the Aga. By the time Sue and Tom came back the cups were finished and lined up in resplendent glory on a worktop. They had very kindly called on Tara's godparents to reassure them I was doing okay and Tom was carrying our bags full of the clothes and stuff that Duncan and Mary thought we might need. Sue spotted the trophies straight away.

"My!" She examined them in surprise. "What a lovely job you've done. I'm ashamed when I think how neglected everything is at that end of the house."

"That was Silas's doing, not yours." Tom squeezed her hand. "Once we get our plans up and running you won't recognize those old rooms."

"I don't want any drastic changes," Sue began.

He tickled her under her chin. "Nothing like that, just some attention and lots of TLC. We'll be able to bring in help, remember. The days of poor old Silas and his refusal to have anyone else around are gone now."

"I suppose so, though I still can't get used to it." Sue gave a tremulous smile, and I knew she was missing the old man. "There's been no response to our adverts so I guess Roger Purley didn't leave any family either, which is very sad."

"I still can't believe you've been asking about the nephew's descendants." Jonah was obviously really angry about it. "Why? What's the point? Roger never came back here, and Silas didn't mention him in the will."

"We've been over this before, Jonah. Silas may have been more upset by his nephew's death than we realized," Sue said. "And I think it's our moral duty to try to make sure there is no one left in Roger's family."

"You're quite right, love, and we've done everything we can." Tom patted her arm soothingly. "The ads have run for several weeks in the States and in Australia and New Zealand. There's not much more we can do."

Jonah didn't comment further but his face turned dark and moody. I tried to lighten the atmosphere by bringing the conversation back to the horse show.

"Maybe next year Ellie will be entering our Open class," Sue said, having listened to our plans for the forthcoming novice jumping. "You'll have to watch it, Jonah, or she'll be beating you and winning that splendid cup."

"You've decided the Garland House Horse Show is going to be an annual event, have you?" Tom asked teasingly.

They all laughed and I was glad I'd changed the subject. They were still mollycoddling me and wouldn't let me help with the outdoor chores, which seemed to be never ending. I spent all day very lazily, playing computer games while they did all the work and feeling guilty because I'd got completely over my fall and could have been helping.

"The doctor said two days' rest." Sue was adamant. "You can watch Jonah lunge your horse this afternoon but you'll have to stay with me when they go out for a hack."

"But—" I started protesting.

"No buts." For such a small person she was very forceful. "I'll teach you how to make really great vegetable soup. And a chocolate pudding."

"Okay." I gave in but knew I'd feel really envious when the other three rode off without me.

The lunge lesson with Aslan was really good, though. Jonah was obviously very experienced and proficient, showing me how to fit the lunging cavesson correctly and providing brushing boots to protect Aslan's legs, a surcingle for his back, and of course the lunging rein and whip.

"It's a good thing to get your horse used to working on the lunge," he explained. "Apart from the training benefits, it provides good exercise during any times you're unable to ride, either through an injury to yourself, like now, or if Aslan ever gets a sore back or anything."

"It would also be a good way to settle him down when he's particularly fizzy, wouldn't it?" I was watching the assured yet gentle way he was handling my pony.

"Exactly," he said and led Aslan to the arena. "Try to get a safe, fenced-in area. If you don't have a school like this, the corner of a field will do, with the two open sides blocked with jumps." I hopped up on the fence and watched the two of them begin.

They were starting with a circle to the left so Jonah held the end of the lunge rein in his left hand with the slack carefully looped back and forth across it. He'd already told me never to secure my hand through the end or to allow the rope to tighten round it.

"The idea is for the horse to move in a true circle around you. Your body moves in the same direction, either walking in a small circle or turning on the spot," he told me, speaking quietly. He then raised his voice to a clear, distinctive command: "Walk on."

Aslan knew what that meant. I watched with interest as Jonah skillfully played out the rein until my pony was walking confidently in a wide circle around him.

"Try to change the pace and direction every ten minutes or so." Jonah didn't take his eyes off Aslan but still managed to talk me through everything they did. "It prevents muscle fatigue and boredom. You're looking for active, rhythmic paces and smooth transitions but as he's new to this we'll only go as far as trot today."

It was great seeing my horse working this way. I was able to appreciate his wonderful conformation and lively, well-balanced action.

"I got in a terrible muddle when I tried this," I confessed. "We started okay, but I couldn't control the rein and the whip at the same time. He just went faster and faster, and I had a real job to make him stop."

"You'll think I'm joking but it's a good idea to practice the technique with a person at the end of the lunge rein until you get the hang of it. Once you're fully competent, your horse will listen to your voice and should come down through his paces obediently. If he doesn't halt when you ask him, walk him toward the barrier, keeping level with his shoulder, and give the command. Very quietly point the whip at his shoulder to discourage him from turning toward you. He should then halt so you go to him and make a really big fuss over him."

He was having no problems himself. When he called "Halt," Aslan did so immediately and stood quietly awaiting the next command. I was dead proud of him and also well impressed with Jonah who was so calm and confident, showing none of the moodiness he sometimes displayed around people. When I heard Tara and Ricky clattering around in the yard behind us I was disappointed that it meant our time in the school was over. I did as Jonah said and made a *huge* fuss over Aslan (no problem there!). The other two had brought Podge, Tolly, and Pharaoh in and, as suspected, I felt very hard done by and sulky as Aslan and I watched them ride off, leaving us like a pair of Cinderellas not allowed to go to the ball.

I explained to Aslan that the other horses had to have their exercise and he'd had his, then turned him back out in the field, smiling indulgently as he immediately lay down and rolled. It's thought that one reason they do that is to get the scent of us humans off them, but I'd rather believe Aslan rolls out of sheer joy and exuberance.

I went back to the house and gave my hands a good scrub in preparation for my cooking lesson. I soon forgot to sulk about not riding, Sue was good company and I'd be taking my horse out the next day and loads of days after, I told myself happily. The first thing to do with the vegetable soup was to wash the vegetables. Sounds simple, but have you ever dealt with stuff that's just come in straight from being dug out of the garden? Well, I'll tell you, it's nothing like the sanitized version you get in supermarket packs; it's a pretty muddy old job. Tom had brought in the box (remembering to take his boots off first this time) and gone back out to do some mulching or some such. There were carrots and sweet corn, tomatoes and onions and some kind of curly greens. I scrubbed away at them with a bristle brush and had to change the dirty water three times just to be able to see the stuff.

I expected to be peeling and chopping for hours but Sue said the skins of carrots and tomatoes had a lot of vitamins and these of course, had not been sprayed with chemicals, so I was to leave them on. She had a big food processor thing that you dropped the clean veggies in, and it whirled round and sliced them all up neatly. I liked the bit where we simmered it all in a big pot on the stove and it started giving out fresh, herby, delicious smells. Tom had also brought in a load of soft fruit, raspberries, strawberries, and blackcurrants, so Sue showed me how to make a Summer Pudding. This involved sloshing soaked bread around happily and watching the lovely purple, pink, and red juice stain it an exciting and appetizing color.

"We don't really need a chocolate sweet as well, do we?" Sue watched me layering it all into a dish.

"Well . . . ," I said coaxingly. "Please."

"All right." She was a very kind and accommodating sort of person. "I'll start mixing the flour and eggs, you melt the chocolate."

"Right." I brought it out of a cupboard. "I'd better try a bit just to make sure it's okay."

"Cheeky," she laughed, then looked up sharply. "Was that the front doorbell?"

"Clanging noise?" I asked helpfully. "Then yes it was."

"Who on earth—" She frowned and brought her floury hands out of the mixing bowl. "Ellie, be a love and see who it is. There's a peephole; look through there and if it's Duncan and Mary bring them on in." I walked out into the hall and approached the heavy front door.

The peephole was slightly taller than my eye and I had to stand on tiptoe. I'm not normally dramatic, but honestly I nearly fell over with shock. A man stood outside, his head turned to one side as he looked up at the house. I had a perfect view of his profile and it was horrible, a great scar running from his forehead, puckering his eyelid and dragging the corner of his mouth downward. It's awful that we're so affected by looks and that my first reaction wasn't one of sympathy but of revulsion, but I just couldn't help it, he looked so sinister. As I stared, unseen to him, he raised his hand and rang the bell again. He certainly wasn't anyone I knew, so I ran back to the kitchen where Sue was drying her hands.

"It's—I don't know who it is and he's—" Words failed me.

She looked at me in surprise. "I'm the one not used to people calling but you needn't look so shocked. Let's go and find out who he is."

She moved briskly to open the door. I stayed just behind her.

"Good morning," she said, "can I help you?"

Seeing him front-on wasn't so bad. The other side of his face was normal and he was smiling, his head tilted to one side and his blue eyes very bright.

"Mrs. Barton?" His voice was soft, with a hesitant stutter and just a hint of an American accent. "I don't suppose you remember me, it's years since we met."

"No, I'm sorry," Sue said, faltering slightly. "Though there is something familiar about you, Mr.—er—"

"Purley." He smiled again and the twisted side of his mouth gave an odd upward twitch. "Roger Purley."

I heard Sue gasp, a deep indrawing of breath, and at the same time I registered what he'd just said. Roger Purley was the name of Silas Crawford's nephew, his one and only relative, whom the Barton family all believed to be dead!

Chapter Seven

For a moment or two we just stood there, Sue and I gaping in astonishment while Roger Purley, his head still tilted to one side, smiled back at us.

"I—I—oh please, come in, Roger." Sue's hands were trembling slightly, I noticed. "Ellie, I think Tom is working in the greenhouse, could you go and fetch him please?"

I went off at a run. Tom looked up in surprise as I came hurtling towards him.

"What's the rush, Ellie? Is everything okay?"

"Yes. No." I was panting quite a bit. "Sue wants you back at the house. There's a—a visitor."

"Really?" Tom wiped his hands on his trousers. "Who's that?"

I hopped from one foot to the other feeling jittery. "It's—he says he's Roger Purley."

"Roger—" He looked as startled as I'd felt. "It can't be—Silas told us he was killed in a car crash."

"His face is all scarred so I guess he has been in a crash." I was practically tugging his arm to get him moving. "Come and see."

Tom, who's very calm and laid-back in an absentminded kind of way, always moves slowly and deliberately, but today he fairly tore through the gardens. We arrived together at the kitchen door and I could practically feel the tension coursing through him. Roger and Sue were sitting at the table drinking coffee; she'd moved the mixing bowl containing the beginnings of our chocolate pudding out of the way.

"Here's Tom." There was great relief in her voice. "Tom, you remember Roger? He's Silas's nephew, we met him when we came for our interview here."

Roger stood up and extended his left hand. I noticed he was holding the right one stiffly against his body.

"Nice to see you again, Tom." The hesitant quality of his voice was very noticeable. "Please excuse the handshake, it's the only one I can manage at present."

Tom returned the greeting, looking dazed.

"I wouldn't have known you," he said. "Of course it's twenty years ago and—"

"And there's this." Roger touched his scarred face self-consciously. "I'm waiting for more plastic surgery but I'm never going to look normal, I guess."

"You sound the same as you used to," Tom said slowly.

Sue broke in at once. "I said that, didn't I, Roger? And I remember you always tilted your head like that. I commented on it to Silas."

"Apparently it's a mannerism I inherited from my father. Uncle Silas always regretted I took after him rather than my mother, who was his sister, of course."

"Of course." Tom looked round the room as if he was hoping for inspiration. "You've—ah—you've got proof of your identity I suppose?"

"I have." Roger bent down and lifted a briefcase onto the table, opening it awkwardly with his left hand. "Passport, birth certificate, driver's license—that's American, as you can see—and I also have other papers if you'd like to see them." Tom and Sue picked up the documents and read them, still with that air of stunned surprise.

"These look fine." Tom turned the paper over. "You must forgive us for seeming so shocked."

"I know how you feel, I was just the same when I saw your advertisement." He pronounced the word the American way. "I realized at once that Uncle Silas had died and as well as saddened I felt so guilty. We were very fond of each other, you know, and I reckon the four years spent here at Garland House were the happiest of my life."

"Really?" Tom looked even more incredulous. "We were under the impression you couldn't wait to leave."

"Ah, that was me being a hotheaded youth." He waved his left hand expressively. "I was just eighteen, you know, when the money from my parents' estate came to me. Dear Uncle Silas wanted me to invest it wisely but I just couldn't wait to do some traveling. Don't get me wrong, I thought Garland House was wonderful, but life with my uncle was so very quiet. He didn't like visitors in those days, but I guess that changed when you two came along."

"No, it stayed the same," Sue said quietly. "We were very fond of your uncle and complied with his—well, some would say eccentricities. He was always kind to us and our sons, and it was his house after all."

"Exactly." Roger rubbed a hand across his face, lingering slightly on the deep furrow of the scar. "He loved it just as I did, that's why I shall be delighted to carry out his wish and continue the family's occupancy of Garland House."

"Live here?" Tom's head came up sharply. "You misunderstand, our advert was to find any possible descendants of Silas so we could give them a share of his money. The house itself has been left to us."

"I can't believe that." He looked truly shocked. "Uncle Silas always said the house would be mine one day. I know we had the falling-out and I know, oh so well, that I should have tried to make amends but all I can do is regret those wasted years. My uncle told me the blood tie of our family was all-important to him so obviously I assumed—" He broke off, his good hand splayed across his eyes, as if to hold back the tears.

Sue leaned forward immediately, her tenderhearted nature obviously touched. "Please don't be distressed, Roger. We placed the notices because we didn't want Silas's family, if there were any, to be disinherited. Your uncle thought you were dead, you see, so there was no mention of you at all in his will."

"I see." The voice, with its oddly hesitant stutter, was broken and barely audible. "I should have realized news of my accident would get back here and I should have contacted him straightaway to let him know I survived. I was too ill, you understand, in a coma for months, then the slow rebuilding of my face, the operations, the pain—"

I saw Tom bite his lip and look at Sue, who was almost crying in sympathy.

"You poor man." She reached out and touched his shoulder gently. "What terrible things you've had to endure. First your parents—"

"Yes, I was only fourteen when they died in that house fire. I was at school and I remember thinking I wished I'd died with them so I wouldn't have the pain of losing them both." At this point he laid his left arm on the table, buried his face in it, and sobbed noisily.

I watched with a kind of fascinated horror. I'd never seen an adult literally cry like a baby. Tom was obviously embarrassed too, clearing his throat repeatedly as if he wanted to speak but couldn't.

"Please don't cry, Roger." Sue's eyes were brimming over with tears. "We'll speak to the lawyers dealing with your uncle's estate and see what can be done."

"You're very kind. I feel you are a kindred spirit who understands what I'm going through." Roger mopped his face vigorously and came up dry-eyed. "Garland House is your home, I understand that, and although I know Uncle Silas originally willed it to me, you are now the legal benefactors."

"Legal yes, but—" Sue turned away and Tom followed her across the kitchen.

He spoke in a low voice, putting his arms all around her, and I could see Roger watching them intently.

"Would you excuse us for a few minutes?" Tom was looking really worried. "My wife and I need to talk. Will you let me know when Jonah and Ricky come back, Ellie, please?"

"Sure." It was practically the first word I'd spoken and it didn't sound like me.

None of this was my business but I was already very fond of the Barton family and empathized with the shock and confusion Roger's appearance had created.

He, meanwhile, helped himself to another cup of coffee and looked around the kitchen. Now I was alone with him I thought I should try to be more normal and speak.

"Has it changed much? Garland House I mean."

"This room's a lot more cheerful than I remember. Who are the two boys Tom just mentioned?"

"Their sons. Jonah's fifteen and Ricky's nearly fourteen. They were born here."

He pursed up his mouth and gave a long whistle, making his scar stretch and pucker. "Were they indeed?"

There came the cheerful clattering of voices and six thumps as boots were removed in the utility room off the kitchen.

"We're back, Ellie," Jonah called, sounding very upbeat. "And something smells great in there. The cooking lesson—" He got to the door and stopped dead, his eyes fixed on Roger Purley, who turned his scarred face to look back at him.

"This—this is Jonah Barton." I felt stupid, introducing them as if it were a formal party or something. "I'll go and tell your mum and dad you're back, Jonah."

It was cowardly but I didn't want to stay and see the gorgeous glow in his eyes replaced by a look of shocked incredulity.

"Hang on, Ellie." Ricky pushed past his brother and came into the room. "Who's this?"

I reminded myself that they weren't used to finding visitors of any kind in the house; their reaction at finding a complete stranger sitting in the kitchen was understandable.

"I'm Roger Purley and you must be Ricky," he said, standing up and offering his left hand. "Oh, and here's another pretty girl; what lucky boys you both are."

I would normally have enjoyed Tara's reaction—she just loves compliments—but after a quick glance at Jonah's lowered brows and thunderstruck expression, I rushed out of the room to find Sue and Tom.

"Ask them both to come in here." Tom was looking very upset. "And if you and Tara don't mind, would you stay with Roger Purley?"

"Sure, that's fine, you all need to talk." I understood perfectly. "I'll make some more coffee, shall I?"

"Thanks, Ellie." Sue's voice was so small I could barely hear her.

I went back to the kitchen, passed on the request, and immediately started fiddling around with the coffeemaker. Tara, as usual, didn't seem at all affected by the bombshell of Roger's appearance, and chatted away to him as if it were a normal, everyday occurrence finding a heavily scarred, supposedly dead person on the doorstep.

"So, what's America like? Daft question, I suppose it depends what bit you live in, it's so huge. Have you been to New York, Mr. Purley?"

"Call me Roger, dear. Yes I've stayed in the Big Apple several times, it's a very exciting city."

"Is that where your accident happened? The one Silas Crawford thought had killed you?" She's not shy and she's not subtle, our Tara.

Roger Purley didn't seem to mind. "No, that was in California, which is a wonderful state. You should go there some time—you too, Ellie."

"Oh, Ellie wants to go to Arizona and live on a horse ranch in the middle of nowhere." Tara wandered to the stove to sniff the big pot of soup. "Mm yummy. Me, I'd rather go to L.A. and meet film stars and live in a house with a pool and all that."

"I'm with you there, kid. I just love a life of luxury."

I made no comment, just poured him some more coffee and wondered cynically how he'd manage to recover so completely from the weeping attack he'd had before.

"I guess the Bartons are having a family conference about me turning up like this," he went on. "I hope it hasn't ruined any plans. What were they going to do with this old house? Sell it I guess."

"No way." Tara helped herself to a biscuit. "Even if they were, why would you arriving change anything?"

"It's a different picture now, isn't it?" He was looking at her but the scarred side of his face was tilted toward me, and I felt a shudder run through me. "I'm the rightful heir after all—Uncle Silas's only blood relation."

"But –" Tara began.

I nipped in quickly. "It's none of our business, is it? You'll have to talk to the family—er—Roger."

"Oh, we can join in surely?" Tara loves to be involved. "Listen, they're coming back. We'll just sit quietly in this corner, Ellie."

"No," I said firmly. "It would be only tactful to leave. We'll go out and see the horses."

I could see she still wanted to stay and practically dragged her out to the back door as the four very subdued Bartons came into the room.

"Tactful!" Tara glared at me as we walked across the field. "I wanted to know what's going on."

"It's a family discussion and we're not family. Ricky will tell you all about it." I said.

"It's not the same as being there. Jonah wasn't just surprised—he was furious. There was practically steam coming out of his ears!"

"That man could do with a few lessons in tact himself," I said heatedly. "Landing here out of the blue and telling them Silas always promised he'd inherit Garland House."

"No! Tara said in shocked delight. "Wait till Sue and

Tom tell your boyfriend that! He'll flatten Roger."

"He's not my boyfriend but he might just do some flat-tening," I agreed, throwing my arms around Aslan's neck and breathing in his lovely comforting smell. "It doesn't help that this bloke is so creepy either."

"I thought he was all right." Tara lay down on the grass. "He looks a bit scary but that's only the scar and he can't help that. He sounds nice and he smiles a lot."

"Only when he's trying to impress." I was thinking of the face I'd glimpsed through the peephole. "When he doesn't know you're looking he's horrible, absolutely hor-rible."Tara pretended to be shocked. "How prejudiced is that! An ugly face does not necessarily denote an ugly spirit. He's probably a very nice man."

"No." I knew I was sounding illogical but that first sight had made a strong, unpleasant impression. "Even if he re-ally is Roger Purley, he's bad, I'm sure of it."

"*If* he really is?" Now Tara sounded genuinely shocked. "You think he's an impostor?"

"He could be. You read about this sort of thing, when someone arrives and says they're the heir but their face is all smashed up. It nearly always turns out they're a fake."

"A fake!" Tara stared up at me. "That can't be right. He said Sue recognized his voice and the way he tilts his head."

"Not much to go on and she only met him once," I reminded her. "And that was twenty years ago. There's something else that's bothering me—something about his injuries—"

Tara put her hand over my mouth to shut me up. "It's so far-fetched—I think you've been reading too many detective novels. This bloke sounds like Roger, moves like Roger, and has all Roger's ID. To me that just adds up to him being Roger."

I shoved her hand away irritably. "You're wrong. He's wrong, he's—he's bad."

"Oh, you're really off on one, aren't you? Nothing to do with the fact your boyfriend looked so rattled when he met Roger?"

"Jonah is not my boyfriend," I yelled, though I secretly liked her calling him that. "And if Roger isn't Roger I'm going to prove it!"

Chapter Eight

"Fine," Tara said. "But don't blame me if everyone thinks you're stark raving mad!"

To be honest, if she'd been right and the whole Barton family had thought that, I might have abandoned the theory, but in fact not everyone disagreed with me. Jonah, when he and Ricky finally emerged from the house, was white with anger and practically spitting dislike of Roger Purley.

"Jonah's totally lost it." Ricky was looking bemused. "Roger's got every proof of identity you could ask for and even knows about a will Silas made leaving Garland House to him, but my brother won't have any of it."

"And you will? That creep is going to take our home away from us! Didn't you hear Mum say even if the old will can't be found Silas's wishes have to be honored? She says it's our moral duty. *Moral's* the last word I'd use in conjunction with Roger Purley."

"Look, why don't you and Ellie go off in a corner somewhere so you can get all your conspiracy theories out of your systems?" Tara's got no time for ranting and raving. "Ricky and I prefer a peaceful life thanks very much."

Jonah looked at me, dark eyes glittering. "You agree with me, Ellie? You don't think we should give Garland House to this creep?"

I took a deep breath. "I'd go farther than that. I don't believe a word this so-called Roger Purley says."

He blinked. "So-called?"

"Ellie's got it in her head that the guy is an impostor, but she's got nothing to back it up except a feeling he's bad and that's based purely on the way he looks."

"That's not it!" I wished I were cleverer with words. "Not because of the scarring, though you have to admit it does make identification conveniently tricky, but with the man himself. When I first saw him he didn't know I was there and he was looking up at the house as if weighing up what it was worth. I could practically see the scheming going on behind his eyes."

"I thought that too," Jonah said eagerly. "I didn't take it to the level of him being an impostor but I could tell straightaway he was a nasty piece of work."

"You're both being unfairly influenced by his appearance," Tara insisted. "That's unkind and melodramatic and no reason to decide to hate him."

"No reason!" Jonah glared at her. "I think there's plenty of reason in the sheer fact of his turning up and saying Garland House should belong to him. If you can't see that you're mad, Tara."

Ricky at once leapt to her defense. "No she's not, so don't take your bad temper out on her. Obviously none of us is happy about the situation but Tara's right, it's no good bleating on about him being bad just because of the way he looks."

"Maybe we haven't explained very well." I didn't want the four of us falling out. "I think that at first glance both Jonah and I saw the real man for a moment. When Sue opened the door and he spoke he was quite different. He smiled and turned on this pleasant manner but I'm sure it was false. It was like he was acting a part."

"You're right." Jonah swung round as if he'd like to kiss me and if I hadn't been so fired up my legs would have turned to squish at the thought. "When I came in he was looking round the kitchen, measuring it up in his mind, but when he saw me his expression changed and he went all charming."

Ricky and Tara didn't look convinced.

"It's not much to go on, is it?" Tara gave a final polish to Podge's snaffle.

We'd taken refuge in the stable yard's tack room because even the weather was reflecting the change Roger Purley's arrival had caused, having grown suddenly dark and gloomy. Big fat spots of rain had driven us in from the paddock, and the somewhat dreary task of tack cleaning suited the mood.

"I mean," Tara went on, "it's more a feeling than a fact-based suspicion isn't it?

"Actually it's not. I've thought and thought about my first glimpse of Roger and I'm sure, pretty sure anyway, that he used his right hand, the so-called injured one, to ring the bell."

"Really, Ellie?" Jonah flashed another one of those admiring glances my way.

"I can't actually swear to it but I think so. Anyway, if we're right about him not being genuine, there's proof out there somewhere. We can ask around the village, find someone who knew Roger better than your parents did."

"Great idea." Jonah was all enthusiasm.

"Mm." Ricky was wavering, though still far from agreeing with us. "That wouldn't hurt, I suppose. I don't fancy doing the asking, though, so what d'you want me to do?"

"If you don't believe us, don't bother," Jonah said shortly, obviously aggrieved by his brother's lack of support.

"You could get him talking," I suggested, trying to keep the peace. "Roger I mean. Tara's great at making people tell her things; maybe he'll slip up and say something about the house that you know the real Roger wouldn't."

"All right, and I'll keep watching to see if he does use his right hand ever, though it's always been sort of clamped to his side, hasn't it? It seems hard to believe he's not real—you should have heard him back there—the bloke must have lived here!"

"The more I think, the more sure I am that Ellie is right." If Jonah had sat any closer I'd have been on his lap. "You two can do what you like. Ellie and I are a partnership from now on—right, Ellie?"

Even though I knew this was really serious stuff I couldn't help enjoying a tingle of anticipation. A partnership with Jonah was, whatever the circumstances, something I felt I could definitely go for. We began straightaway, walking into the nearby village to find out if there were any locals who'd known Roger Purley during his four-year stay at Garland House. I didn't have a clue how to go about it and just followed Jonah dumbly into the little store in the High Street. To my surprise we were met with a very friendly greeting from a cheerful-looking lady behind the till.

"Hello, Jonah, nice to see you. How's your ma and pa?"

"Fine thanks, Mrs. Dee." Jonah smiled back.

"They'll be busy I expect, now they've started to expand the gardening side. Your dad's told me to come along and see the setup now old Silas is gone. This was the first shop in these parts to sell your organic veggies and it's going great."

"That's terrific, thanks very much. Mrs. Dee, you've lived here for quite a while, haven't you?"

"All my life," she boasted, busily dusting an already immaculate shelf. "And I'm a bit older than twenty-one, that's all I'm saying."

We both laughed politely and Jonah said, "So you must have known Roger Purley, who came to live at Garland House about twenty-five years ago?"

She stopped dusting and thought deeply. "D'you know, I'd forgotten about him. He was a nephew or cousin of Silas's, wasn't he?"

"Nephew. His mother was Silas's sister, but she and her husband died in a fire."

"Poor lad. I remember now, felt very sorry for him losing them like that and then being dumped with a cranky old uncle."

"That's great! I mean, I'm glad you knew him," Jonah said excitedly.

"Oh, I didn't. Saw him once or twice to say good morning but that was it. Old Silas never came into the village, as you know, and the boy was either away at school or holed up at Garland House. Nobody round here got to know him and he went off for good—don't know when—before your parents' time anyway."

Jonah's face fell and I tried to think of something. "What about the cook at Garland House in those days, Mrs. Dee? Is she still around?"

"No, she wasn't a local, I think she went back to the coast somewhere when she retired. There used to be a gardener, though, come to think of it—Billy Fellowes, real old villager he was."

"Would he talk to us?" Jonah was very anxious. "We just want to ask—"

"He died years back, love." Mrs. Dee patted his arm kindly. "Your folks could tell you that. Billy Fellowes died, so the gardens were all neglected. Then the cook retired so Silas had to employ some help. All I can say is, he was real lucky getting you Bartons. The difference your ma and pa must have made to his life, putting up with his weird ways and looking after him so well."

"We liked him," Jonah said, trying not to show how disappointed he was. "Thanks very much for talking to us, Mrs. Dee. I'll just have a bar of chocolate for now."

He paid her and we left, wondering what to do now that our investigations had come to such an abrupt halt.

"Here you are, Ellie." Jonah handed me the chocolate. "Thanks for supporting me. It was worth a try, I guess."

I broke the bar and handed him half and decided to keep the wrapper forever. "You're not giving up? There must be something else we can do."

"I can't think what." He kicked a pebble moodily. "You heard her. There's no one alive here who knew Roger. I thought there'd be people he went to the local school with, mates he had in the village and so on, but if he went off to school and if Mrs. Dee can't remember much about him it's hopeless. She's very nice but dead nosy, finds out everything about everybody."

"Except Silas and his household." I bit into the chocolate thoughtfully. "So we're going to have to ask farther afield. Roger's school is the obvious place. They must have records, registers of pupils' names or even teachers who were there when he was fourteen."

"Brilliant!" He gave me that glowing look again, and I went as soft and gooey as the chocolate I was eating. "Um—how do we go about that?"

"Duncan and Mary have a computer. I'll search on the Internet. Can you find out the name and address of the school?"

"Yeah, Mum will know, I'm sure."

We made our way back to the house, hoping that by now Roger would have gone, but as soon as we walked through the back door we could hear him. His distinctive voice was really quite pleasant, but Jonah wasn't at all happy at hearing it.

"When's he going to push off?" he hissed.

I shook my head and went on into the kitchen. Roger was still sitting at the table, now happily slurping a bowl of my excellent organic vegetable soup. Ricky and Tara were tucking in too, their eyes wide and interested as they listened to the travel tales Roger was recounting. Sue and Tom, still pale and subdued looking, were standing listlessly at the sink, looking out the window at the view of the gardens they loved so much.

With a palpable effort Sue turned to smile at us. "You're a bit late for lunch but I made sure these three saved you some. Your soup's really good, Ellie."

"Thanks." It did smell great but I wasn't hungry, despite only having eaten half a chocolate bar. "Maybe I'll try some tonight."

"If it's still on offer at suppertime put me down for another bowlful." Roger smiled his crooked grin at me. "It's delicious, Ellie."

"Glad you like it." I bared my teeth sarcastically in return; there was no way I would give him a genuine smile.

"You're staying?" Jonah stared at him incredulously and Sue made a nervous movement.

"Yes, Roger is to be our guest for a while. It's the least we can do for Silas's nephew." Tom spoke quietly but the meaning was clear—*back off now, Jonah!*

Jonah opened his mouth to speak, closed it again, then turned and went back through the boots room and out of the house. For a moment I hesitated, not wanting to be rude to the Bartons, but then I swear I saw a malicious gleam in Roger's eye so I wheeled round and followed. He was striding toward the stable block, his long legs going so fast I'd never catch him.

"Jonah!" I called and he stopped immediately. I ran to him and said rather breathlessly, "Partners, remember? We're a partnership, and I'm on your side."

The tense set of his shoulders relaxed and his dark, shuttered expression lightened a little. "You don't have to be, you've only just met me and we're thrown into this shambles of a situation. I'd never have believed my parents could be so stupid!"

"They're not. They're being considerate and reasonable and kind, which is exactly the sort of people they are. We've got an advantage on them, you and me, because we've both caught sight of Roger when his guard was down. Sue and Tom are dealing with a man who seems genuinely to love Garland House and his uncle and is full of remorse for not being here. Roger puts on the act beautifully and he's done his research, tells nice anecdotes about Silas and growing up here."

"He must be a total phony," Jonah said. "No one ought

to be taken in by him. He's—he's—" Words failed him.

"Like I say, we're pretty sure but the rest of your family isn't. Tara thinks he's okay, and she's as sharp as a tack generally. Roger has to deal with solicitors tomorrow, though, and he won't find it as easy to hoodwink them. With a bit of luck they'll have all sorts of evidence to trip him up."

That seemed to cheer Jonah up a bit, and he agreed to simmer down until Roger had been to his appointment with the Bartons' lawyers. The rest of the day was still fraught with tension, though, as Jonah tried to stay out of the way, making a huge effort not to start any rows but doing an awful lot in the way of brooding silences. I was taking a different approach, being polite and determinedly cheerful with everyone, while watching Roger like a hawk on heavy surveillance duty. Ricky and Tara were both aware of what was going on and did their best to help me, asking Roger loads of questions so I could make mental notes and catch him out saying something wrong. The guy was brilliant, though, and I actually don't mean that as a compliment. He seemed so relaxed and easygoing about answering and quite often he'd say with engaging candor,

"D'you know, I can't recall a single thing about that. I wonder if the injuries to my head have muzzed up my memory, or is it just that it's such a long time ago and I was only a kid at the time?"

"You were our age!" Tara said. "Though come to think of it my mum's only a year older than you and she says she can't remember being a teenager at all!"

"Your mum sounds a sweetie, just like her gorgeous daughter," Roger said. I saw Jonah in the background making violent vomiting actions at the blatant flattery.

I kept up my surveillance all evening but was just about ready to admit defeat when I went upstairs to bed. Roger hadn't faltered, had given no more of those sneaky, avaricious looks at his surroundings, given no reason whatsoever to doubt everything about him was genuine, and had held his right hand awkwardly tucked into his side the whole time. In my room, I started getting undressed, then realized I'd left a book Jonah had lent me downstairs. Tara was in the bathroom so without calling out or anything I padded back down the stairs. The book was on an arm of the sofa, and I entered the room noiselessly to get it. There, with his back to me, was Roger, and he was reaching out for a wine bottle Tom had opened earlier. The arm that was outstretched was his right one, and this time there was no doubt whatsoever—he was using the one that was supposed to be so badly damaged he could barely move it at all!

Chapter Nine

I didn't make a sound, just backed out of the room and legged it back upstairs to find Jonah in his room.

"You're certain this time?" He quickly put a sweatshirt on.

"Absolutely." I was agog to get back there.

We rushed (silently) to the living room and peered in. Roger was sitting in an armchair, reading a paper and drinking his wine, which was now, I was disappointed to see, held in his left hand.

He looked up. "Hi you two. You've come back to bid me good night, have you?"

This was obviously a jibe at the fact Jonah and I had pointedly not spoken to him at all.

"No," I said, hurriedly concocting a cunning plan to make him use his right arm again. "We—er—we won-

119

dered if there was any wine left."

He raised his crooked eyebrows. "Bit young to be drinking, aren't you? There's a drop if you want it."

"No, you have it. I—just wanted to take the empty bottle to the kitchen."

"Really?" The eyebrows went higher. "That's very tidy of you. I'll finish it off then."

I held my breath as he placed the glass carefully on a table and turned toward the bottle. With a typically clumsy movement he stretched out the arm farther from it, the left one, and poured the last few dregs. "Thank you Ellie." His right arm was again cradled against his side. "And Jonah, of course."

Jonah glowered at him from under dark, lowered brows then turned on his heel and marched out. I grabbed the book I'd left and followed him, wishing hard I'd been cleverer and a lot more cunning.

"I'm really sorry." I timidly put out a hand to touch Jonah's sleeve. "I was positive he used his bad arm just now. D'you think I've put him on his guard?"

Jonah stopped and made an obvious effort to smile. "It's

not your fault, he's just unbelievably tricky. He's got to slip up some time. All we have to do is keep on trying to catch him."

The next morning, as soon as the feeding and milking chores were finished, Sue and Tom, looking quite unfamiliar in their smart going-to-town clothes, set off in their car with Roger. Tara and Ricky were still deeply involved with something in the vegetable garden and had planned to make another trip to the nature reserve when they finished. Jonah and I headed straight for the schooling ring with Aslan.

"We'll give him a short spell on the lunge." Jonah was expertly coiling the long rein into loops across his hand. "It'll make him concentrate and calm him down before you start riding. You're sure you're okay?"

"Yes," I said, a bit shortly because I'd said over and over again to him and to Sue that I was perfectly all right with no aftereffects from my fall. I really, really wanted to ride today.

"Okay." He grinned at me to show he understood my irritation and asked Aslan to walk on.

This time, once he got my pony responding well, he let me take the lunge line, standing near me so he could help and advise. It was brilliant, working Aslan from the ground, and I was concentrating so hard I barely registered the fact that Jonah was close enough that I could feel his breath on my cheek. No, I lie; I was perfectly aware and enjoyed it a lot. Once I'd finished lunging and rewarded him for being so good, I tacked him up and started the lesson proper.

"The technique required for jumping a show course successfully is a combination of agility and speed," Jonah told me. "You and your pony are naturally talented, very bold and very fast, but you have to learn to produce a sensible, controlled round in a consistent rhythm."

Thinking of the way Aslan and I went thundering up to the fences and ditches we jumped when out on a hack, I made a grimace.

"You can do it," Jonah said, laughing at my face. "I want to see you taking several different layouts without letting Aslan get faster and faster until he's out of control. That's a typical novice mistake."

He was right about that—the few times I'd tried to get my pony round the simple clear round course at local shows, we'd started off fine but ended galloping madly round the enclosure flattening some fences and completely bypassing others. Today, though, with Jonah's calm, informative presence in the middle of the school, we were soon jumping the last fence as successfully as the first. Jonah was particularly pleased to see us dealing well with the doubles he'd built.

"Provided they're the right height and the distances are correct, they do a lot to encourage good jumping by training the horse's eye and teaching him to think and concentrate."

I was surprised at how much of the last two I was doing as well, and at how tiring it was.

"You've both done brilliantly." Jonah's eyes were as warm as toast. "Make a big fuss over him and give him a long rein so he can stretch and cool down."

I felt very exhilarated and wished we were going straight out on the hack we'd planned for later. Jonah wanted to school Pharaoh first. though. so after rubbing Aslan down and leaving him to rest in the stable I went back to watch the superb black horse being put through his paces. The two of them were a joy to watch. and I happily trundled around building fences up and clapping in admiration as they soared athletically over every obstacle. We were so deeply involved and enjoying ourselves that we forgot to fret about the Bartons' trip to their solicitors with Roger. It wasn't till we heard their car pulling up at the front of the house that we thought about it.

"Help me untack Pharaoh and we'll go and see if those lawyers have told Mr. I-don't-think-so Purley where to get off."

I found myself silently praying that the lawyers had, indeed, been able to expose Roger as a fake and left the yard hoping against hope it was true. We knew as soon as we walked through the back door that it wasn't so. Roger's slightly hesitant voice was raised a little as he handed out more of his outrageous brand of flattery.

"So I said to them, don't you worry, I know Ricky and Tara will help me search and they're such a couple of bright kids they'll find it in no time."

"Find what?" Jonah sounded even surlier than ever as we went into the kitchen and I saw a flash of annoyance pass between his parents.

"Our lawyers don't have the will Silas made all those years ago," Sue said, her eyes worried as she watched her eldest son. "But Roger remembers the day his uncle wrote it, so the paper has to be somewhere in the house."

"Silas wrote it here?" Jonah said in disbelief. "Hardly likely when he must have known it needed to be counter-signed by two witnesses."

"Jonah!" Tom began.

Roger held up his hand peacemaking style. "The boy's quite right, Tom, you have very clever children I'm pleased to see. There were two witnesses, Jonah, so it was all perfectly legal."

"Are you sure? We all know Silas would never have visitors at Garland."

"No need, no need. One was the cook, Mrs. Babbage she was called, funny old soul but quite able to witness a signature. The other was a real old bumpkin, used to come in a couple of times a week to do the garden. I can't remember his name—"

"Fellowes, Billy Fellowes," Tom said, glaring hard at Jonah. "He died before we got here but you're quite right about him, Roger. Jonah, I think we need to have a word."

He left the room abruptly and Jonah followed, slouching sullenly. There was an embarrassed silence and Tara said quickly, "Let's go and finish up in the garden, Ricky. D'you want to come, Ellie?"

"No, I'll wait for Jonah," I said, turning my back pointedly on Roger Purley.

Yeah, I know, childish, but I completely empathized with the way Jonah felt about the lying, conniving impostor and I wanted him, and everyone else, to know. Tara shrugged. We're usually pretty well attuned but she just wasn't with me on this one. She and Ricky left. Sue looked at me, probably wondering whether it was in order to tell me off too but deciding against it. I silently helped her make some sandwiches while she made rather stilted conversation with Roger who soon, to her evident relief, went off to read his paper in another room.

"This is so awful." She lay down the knife and looked

at me. "I know Jonah's upset, we're all terribly upset, but the right thing has to be done and letting Roger have the house is the right thing. It's what Silas wanted after all—"

"You've only got Roger's word for that," I pointed out. "And he's—"

"He's scum!" Jonah strode back in. "And if he's eating with us again I'm going out. You coming, Ellie?"

"Yes." I hurriedly finished the last sandwich.

Sue sighed deeply, put some in a bag, and added two drinks and some apples.

"You and Jonah take these and go for a picnic somewhere. And please, Ellie, try to talk some sense into him." *Sense!* I thought crossly. *Jonah and I are the only ones with sense round here.*

Our horses seemed a little surprised to be tacked up again but very keen to go out, and as soon as we emerged from the wood and saw the beautiful moorland stretching into the distance I felt my own spirits lift too. It was a beautiful day and after yesterday's rain everything looked freshly washed, from the clear, pale blue of the sky to the fragrant colors of heather, gorse, and moss. Soon we were galloping along a broad path of springy turf, and it was wonderful feeling the soft air in my face and the surging, powerful speed of the horse beneath me. We rode farther this time, picking our way carefully across the rocky bed of a stream and cantering joyfully up a steep hill covered in the soft green fronds of waving ferns. Then the land dipped away again and soon we were walking beside a river, whose sparkling waters cut a snaking silver path through the landscape.

We dismounted and unsaddled, tethering the horses loosely to a tree so they could rest and nibble at the short, sweet grass. Jonah and I shared the sandwiches, and I thought I'd never tasted anything so good. Mind you, you could practically eat sawdust in surroundings like those and it would taste like nectar. (Okay, I don't know what nectar tastes like but you know what I mean.) Jonah was enjoying himself too, the harsh set of his mouth softened as the tension in his jaw relaxed.He stretched out and gave his last bit of apple to Pharaoh and I did the same for Aslan. "I could stay here for ever."

"It might be a good idea at that," I said cautiously. "Your

mum and dad are getting totally fed up with our attitude toward Roger. The lawyers obviously didn't find anything to suggest he was a fake.

"Stupid #@%&$." He swore. "They checked all his papers, including signatures, even phoned the California hospital where he was taken after the accident and still they didn't come up with anything."

"Really?" I stared at him. "That's pretty conclusive surely?"

He groaned and rolled over onto his stomach. "Don't you start believing him, Ellie."

"I won't, I don't." I made myself recall that first, frightening glimpse of Roger as he looked up at the house. "But if solicitors can't find evidence to show he's a fake, what chance do we have?"

"We have to try." He clenched his fists. "Oh, he's being really clever, telling Mum and Dad they can stay as long as they like, that Dad can carry on working the gardens, that everything will stay the same, but it won't."

"You think he'll change once Garland House is legally his?"

He looked cynical. "Don't you?"

"Yes," I said slowly, trying to remember something. "He told Tara he loved a life of luxury and ease, not the sort of style your parents go in for at all."

"Exactly." He looked so gloomy again I had to try to cheer him up.

"Now, laddie," I said in refined tones. "Do not pull that worried face or the wind will change and you'll stay like that."

He stared at me in astonishment for a moment, then grinned. "You sound like someone's elderly maiden aunt."

"That's right." I nodded. "It's a great-great of Tara's— Aunty Jane. It's my best impression, I sound exactly like her."

"I'd be overwhelmed if I happened to know her." He was intrigued now. "Do someone I would recognize."

I immediately reeled off a very good Sue, an amazing Tara, and a passable Ricky.

"You're brilliant! Anyone else?"

I thought for a bit then gave out two barks, one deep and baying, the other high-pitched and slightly hysterical.

Pharaoh immediately lifted his head and stared at me. Jonah roared with laughter.

"He thinks you've got Drummer and Sidney hidden somewhere. It's okay, Pharaoh mate; they're both at home helping in the garden."

I finished with my by now famous duck impersonation, quacking so loud and long that Aslan, his head tilted curiously to one side, moved forward and nudged me in the stomach.

"I think he's had enough," I laughed, really happy I'd managed to cheer Jonah up.

We rode home, taking some of the route at a slow, lazy pace so we wouldn't get back too soon. The closer we got, the more the problem of proving Roger was a phony started bugging me, and when we turned into the yard and I saw he was standing there my pent-up feelings ran riot. Roger was outside one of the stables, his head turned away from me so the scarred side of his face was in profile. He seemed to be looking at Charlie who, in typical feline fashion, was stretched out against the wall enjoying the warm sun. Roger's distorted mouth was downturned, and I was sure I could see a hard glitter in the puckered eye as he moved slowly toward the cat. The picture he made was so chilling that a terrible thought sprang into my brain.

"He's going to kick Charlie! Roger's going to hurt poor Charlie!"

Chapter Ten

If I'd had time to think I'd have acted more rationally but once more Roger looked so evil, I just acted on instinct. I slid quickly from Aslan's back and ran forward. My lovely pony followed at a brisk trot and when Roger looked up it was to see the two of us bombing straight for him. He sidestepped nervously and I ducked behind him, scooping Charlie into my arms. I swear I hadn't given a thought that Aslan would keep going, determined to stay close to me. Just as I picked up the cat, Ricky's head suddenly appeared inside the stable door. At the same time Roger fell noisily to the ground, letting out a tremendous groan as he crumpled.

"What the—?" Ricky peered with astonishment over the door at the prone figure. "Did you just get your horse to knock Roger over?"

"Of course not!" I grabbed my pony's reins with my free hand. "Aslan wouldn't do that."

Ricky quickly came out and helped Roger to his feet. "Are you okay, Roger? What happened?"

"I think you saw what happened. Ellie ran behind me and her horse just kept going, took me completely off my feet because, of course, I couldn't fend him off with my injured hand."

"Rubbish!" I was furious with myself because I'd messed up really badly. "I was running to pick up Charlie, and Aslan didn't touch you. You must have tripped."

"I assure you I didn't but I'm not one to make a fuss. Ricky saw your horse knock me over, didn't you, Rick?"

"I—I expect Ellie and Aslan were playing one of their funny little games," Ricky said, slightly desperately. "It wouldn't have been deliberate."

"It was just an accident," Jonah confirmed as he joined us. "No big deal."

"Oh well." Roger dusted himself down left-handedly, wincing dramatically. "I'm not badly hurt, so no harm done."

We watched him leave the yard in silence then Ricky said, "I hope he doesn't tell Mum and Dad about that. They're already pretty annoyed at the way you two are treating him."

"Annoyed!" Jonah was immediately ready to burst into flames. "What's the matter with you all? The guy's a creep and most likely a fake!"

"Listen, Jonah, the lawyers have done a lot of checking and so far everything Roger has said is true. He was in that horrific car crash and he did sustain all the injuries he told us about. Fractured skull, multiple facial wounds, broken ribs, right arm and toes, plus burns that required skin grafts."

"None of that proves he's Roger Purley. Car smashes happen all the time and he's obviously been in one but—"

"Not just in any one but *the* one, the one Silas was told about. A friend of Roger's was helping him move using a rental truck when they smashed through a barrier on a California highway. Roger was dragged unconscious from the wreck and his friend was killed. Because the truck was rented by R. Purley, it was assumed at first that that's who the dead driver was; that was why Silas was informed his nephew had died. Roger didn't gain consciousness for weeks and afterward was too ill to contact anyone. All the hospital records prove that Roger Purley is exactly who he says he is. So give us all a break and accept it, will you?"

"No I won't. You haven't seen him, weighing the house up, working out what everything's worth in hard cash. All that stuff about loving his uncle and Garland is a complete load of—"

Ricky sighed heavily and looked at me. "And you think so too, Ellie?"

"Yes," I said strongly, but a wave of despair washed over me. I thought of telling them about seeing him pick up the wine bottle with his right hand the night before, but stopped myself. If lawyers who had access to all sorts of evidence believed Roger was telling the truth, how on earth were we going to prove otherwise?

Ricky made a gesture of defeat. "Tara and I said we'd help him look for the will making the house Roger's. Now don't go ballistic—" He backed up as Jonah moved menacingly toward him. "We think you've both got a bad case of wishful thinking, but if we see anything that makes us change our minds we'll let you know. Roger won't want you two anywhere near him after his brush with Aslan but Tara and I can rummage around in desks and stuff and keep an eye on him at the same time."

"Don't do us any favors," his brother snarled as he led Pharaoh into his box to be untacked. "Ellie and I will get some proof—we don't need you." *Actually we do*, I thought as I trailed off to sort out Aslan. *I can't see how we're going to do this on our own.*

Jonah was already so depressed I didn't say it out loud, just told myself fiercely to get my brain in gear and do some serious thinking. Roger, Tara, and Ricky embarked on their first session of will hunting later that day. We were due to return to Critchell Farm and although I didn't want to leave Jonah, I was secretly relieved I wouldn't have to spend all my evenings waiting for Roger to make a slip. Tara, riding home with me, started on the subject straight-away.

"I'd love him to be proved a phony." She took her feet out of the stirrups and lolled back. "I just adore what Tom's done to the gardens and although Roger says it'll all go on exactly the same once he's owner of Garland, I can't help thinking he's bound to make changes."

"Of course he is." I was glad she and I were at least discussing it, even if from different angles. "Where are the Bartons going to live anyway? Are they staying on as Roger's guests or something?"

"No, they're going to use the money Silas left to buy a house in the village. Roger's really rich with all the money from his parents so he's got enough to keep running Garland."

"Why doesn't he push off for now and stay in a hotel then?" I knew Jonah would be pleased if he did that.

"Because he loves the house so much, never wants to leave it again."

I was amazed the way they all believed it. As Jonah said, how come he'd stayed away so long then?

I changed the subject slightly. "How did the famous will hunting go?"

"I know you don't believe there is one and that Roger's just pretending to search for appearance's sake but that's not true honestly, El. We started in the study Silas used to use and Roger was really crawling about, emptying cupboards and searching all the drawers. He didn't stop for two hours."

"And what did you find?"

"Nothing really. A few funny little containers, snuffboxes apparently, Silas collected them at one time. There was the usual bunch of papers, receipts and stuff, but no personal letters or photos. I thought that was odd but Ricky said Silas didn't do personal."

"Sounds dull," I said shortly.

She twisted round and glared at me. "It is and I'm only doing it as a favor to you. Rick and I said we'd keep an eye on Roger, and we are."

I felt a bit guilty. "Thanks, Tara, I'm sorry we're clashing over this. I do appreciate what you're doing and I don't want us to fall out."

"Me neither." She smiled straight at me, and I felt better.

"Come for a ride with us tomorrow," I said. "And I promise Jonah and I won't keep on about the Roger thing."

"Okay," she agreed. "But don't expect Podge and me to keep up with you two—it's like following a pair of race-horses!"

She was right. The next day, once all four horses were warmed up, Jonah and Pharaoh led us in a long gallop. While I was reveling in the amazing sensation of speed and power, I was also aware we were leaving Podge and Tolly farther and farther behind. Ricky and Tara didn't seem to mind, though, just cantered up to join us when we finally stopped. We walked the next mile or so in perfect harmony, talking about anything and everything except Roger Purley. Jonah and his brother had come to some kind of truce about not discussing the scarred man, which meant the atmosphere was lighter and a lot more friendly. I told myself it was almost back to the carefree way we'd been when we first met but I knew that just under the surface the Roger situation boiled and fermented like an explosion waiting to happen. Still, I was happy to be out on the beautiful moor and when I realized we were approaching the lovely spot by the river where Jonah and I had picnicked, I immediately suggested we swim.

"What—in our underwear?" Tara said.

I pretended to bash her. "Swim the horses, you donkey! We can take their saddles off, it's not too deep and there's no fast current."

"We used to do it quite often, didn't we, Jonah?" Ricky sounded enthusiastic. "Only Pharaoh's a bit of a sissy about getting wet so we haven't been in for ages."

"He'll be okay with Aslan around. They're so competitive, once Pharaoh sees us going in he'll want to swim too." I couldn't wait and leapt off my pony's back straightaway.

If it had been just Tara and me I'd have stripped out of my pants, but I wasn't about to in front of Jonah and Ricky. After taking off Aslan's saddle, I just rolled up my jeans and vaulted onto his smooth, chestnut back.

"Show-off!" Tara pulled a face then groaned as Ricky took a handful of Tolly's mane and did the same. "Someone's gonna have to give me a leg-up, I can never get onto Podge bareback."

"I'm not sure I can do it on Pharaoh either. He's too tall." Jonah looked so downcast I had to laugh.

"Can't be good at everything, love," I said in a very good

imitation of his mum's voice and he looked up at me and joined in the laughter.

I slid off Aslan, helped him up on the black horse, then flipped Tara easily onto the round gray back of Podge.

"All set?" I vaulted back aboard my patiently waiting pony and urged him forward.

Aslan just loves the water. At first he just stood hock-deep in the river, his fine head lowered to sniff and savor the cool, clear shallows. Jonah tried to follow, encouraging Pharaoh with everything he had: legs, voice, and seat. The big black pranced around nervously, putting one hoof then another in the water then hopping back as if the gentle flow had nipped him.

"I'll go next with Tolly, shall I?" Ricky was grinning, obviously enjoying seeing his brilliant rider of a brother having no success for once.

"I feel such an idiot." Jonah looked as though he'd have picked the horse up and carried him if he could.

Tolly walked calmly past him and Ricky and I sat a few meters from the bank and watched Pharaoh's performance, trying not to laugh too much. After several minutes I suggested Tara and Podge come in too.

"If we're all in the river and start swimming away from you, Pharaoh will want to follow. He thinks he's herd leader so I'm sure he won't let us go without him."

I moved Aslan forward and soon he was swimming, powerful shoulders thrusting as he forged strongly through the water. Within seconds my jeans were soaked, of course, but it didn't matter, they'd dry in the sun and the swimming was absolutely worth it. Tara shrieked a bit when the cold water first touched her, but soon she too was laughing with the sheer joy of the experience. Ricky and Tolly had a slightly unusual action, with Ricky crouched like a jockey as his bay horse struck out with an odd, choppy motion a bit like a mechanical toy driven by an erratic motor. Pharaoh stayed on the bank, stamping his feet and whinnying anxiously as his little band swam farther and farther away, while Jonah still tried everything he could to join us.

"Come on, Pharaoh!" I yelled, turning just in time to see the black horse make a sudden, desperate plunge toward us. Unfortunately it took Jonah completely by surprise, and instead of staying put and riding into the deeper reaches of the river he fell in headfirst, coming up quickly to swim alongside his horse's shoulder.

"You're supposed to be on top," Ricky shouted unkindly. Jonah said something in reply but luckily all we heard was a load of mildly infuriated spluttering.

Pharaoh, now that he was in the water, was absolutely loving it, moving strongly toward us while Jonah did his best to keep up. As they approached I leaned over and caught the horse's reins, bringing him close to Aslan's side.

"Thanks, Ellie," Jonah gasped, swimming the last few strokes then sliding gratefully onto Pharaoh's wetly gleaming back. "Pharaoh you're a—a—"

"Now, now, no bad language," I said in Tom's gentle manner. We all laughed again and carried on swimming our horses.

It was a brilliant morning and so wonderful to be out there having a good time that no one wanted to go home.

"I have to." Ricky looked at Tara. "Dad and I are replacing some of the old nesting boxes in the nature reserve today."

"Ooh yeah, and he said I could go along as well." She

looked down at her soaking-wet jeans. "I'll have to back to the house first to change."

"We've got time, I'll come with you." Ricky was certainly keen on her, I thought, and silently hoped Jonah felt the same way about me.

"Will you stay, Ellie?" His dark eyes were hopeful. "We could ride a bit longer."

"Sure I will," I said as casually as I could.

"We'll soon dry off in the sun." He ran his hand through his wet hair. "If that's okay with you?"

"Okay." I was being ultra-cool but I don't think I fooled anyone for a minute.

Ricky and Tara set off for Garland House while Jonah and I rode peacefully onward, crossing another long tract of moorland where birds sang and bees hummed blissfully in and out of the heather bells, rocking them so they gave out their tiny, dry tinkle. We trotted and cantered, hopped easily over a couple of shrub jumps and some ditches, and came to another stream where the sun, high in the sky now, gave the broad ripples a dappled, molten gleam. Jonah dismounted and dragged a few logs around to make a mini jumping course.

"Pretend you're entering the ring here." He pointed. "Then take one, two, three, and four in that order and canter on to stream, making it number five."

Aslan, who was enjoying himself so much he was positively bouncing, snorted eagerly and tried to rush at the first log.

"Remember your lessons," Jonah said. I brought my pony's speed down and curved him away to do a few dressage steps.

Once I had his attention I made my approach again and this time could feel the perfect shape of his outline as he accepted the bit and looked properly at the staggered row of jumps. Each takeoff was spot-on, as we landed we were already turning to make the correct approach for the next, and when we finally soared over the stream to land neatly on its far bank I knew Jonah would be really pleased with us. I was proud too. I know they were only small jumps but we'd handled them properly with none of our former out-of-control madness. Jonah followed, looking incredibly gorgeous on the shining ebony horse as they cantered the course effortlessly.

"Well done." He landed beside me and leaned over to pat Aslan's neck. "You're a couple of stars, aren't you?"

It had been a long ride, and to cool the horses down and finish the drying off our clothes we dropped back to a sedate walk as we finally left the moor behind us. I had no idea where we were; this wasn't the route back we'd taken before, but it was lovely to be traveling along a pretty country lane chatting easily to Jonah, who'd relaxed so much he seemed to have forgotten all about the problem of Roger Purley. Suddenly, though, the line of his mouth hardened, and he stood in his stirrups to peer through the trees.

"It's him!" He pointed and I moved in to see.

Through the branches I could see a road and a pub, and in the parking lot of the pub, there, talking to a man in a dark business suit, was Roger Purley. He was carrying some papers rolled together in a long tube, and I could see he was indicating at them as if describing something to the other man. They started walking together toward the pub, a quiet, nondescript little place set a good way back from the lane.

"He's up to something!" Jonah's voice was urgent and it was no surprise to me when I found we were riding our horses quietly around the back of the pub, with the definite purpose of spying on Roger and the man in black.

Chapter Eleven

The trees and shrubs around the pub provided good cover, keeping us completely out of sight from anyone inside.

"I need to get closer," Jonah said, sliding down from Pharaoh's saddle and handing me his reins.

Running swiftly, he soon reached the building and flattened himself against the wall, edging cautiously toward a low, broad window. I saw his dark head turn to look inside and knew by the slump of his shoulders he was disappointed at what he saw. He stood still for a moment or two, then moved off again, disappearing round the side of the pub. A few minutes passed and I began to worry that he'd gone inside and confronted Roger, causing another row that would get us into more trouble. It was a relief to see him reappear, running rapidly back to take Pharaoh's reins again.

"We have to wait." All the tension our glorious morning had dissipated was back, and his mouth was again set in a hard, straight line. "They're sitting right at the back, too far from the window for me to see those papers or hear what they're talking about."

"So what are we waiting for?" I calmed Aslan, who was beginning to fidget.

"My mate's sister, Mandy, has a holiday job here as a waitress. I went round the back and asked her if she could hover about and find out what Roger and that bloke are doing."

"And she agreed?" I wasn't surprised really. I expect most girls would do anything Jonah asked.

"Sure." He was peering through the trees. "She's doing it straightaway. We won't have to wait long."

True enough, after five minutes or so a girl came out of the pub's back door and started trotting toward us.

"Jonah!" she said. "I went up and asked if they wanted to order any food but they're only having a drink so I couldn't hang around."

"Could you see what the papers were, though?" Jonah

asked eagerly.

"They're some kind of plans, architect's drawings maybe. The man with the scar stopped talking when I got near but I heard the other one say, 'So it's a definite deal then?'"

"A deal," Jonah said thoughtfully. "Could the plans have been of Garland House, Mandy?"

"They could be." Mandy was giving me the once-over, trying to decide if I was the girlfriend I guess. "Sorry I can't tell you any more, Jonah, I mustn't stay in the bar any longer because I'm supposed to be in the dining room round the back."

"You've been great." Jonah flashed his fabulous smile. I bet she went all squirmy.

We watched her return to the pub, then Jonah climbed back into his horse's saddle and we made our way through the trees back to the quiet lane beyond.

"A deal," Jonah said again, obviously thinking hard. "What kind of deal?"

I shook my head. "It could be a business thing of Roger's, but what I want to know is why come out here to discuss it? Roger already treats Garland as if it's his own house, so why didn't he arrange for the man in the suit to meet him there?"

"Good question, Ellie. He must be up to something or why would he be hiding it from Mum and Dad? I'm going straight home to tell them."

"Better not," I said cautiously "We don't actually have proof of anything, do we? It might be better to tackle Roger first. We've got the element of surprise on our side because he won't have any idea we saw him back there."

"That's true. If I can spring it on him—*We know about the house plans and the deal you've been making*, that sort of thing—he won't have time to cook up any of his stories."

It wasn't great, but though we talked about it all the way home we didn't come up with anything better. The horses were nicely cooled down so after a good rubdown they were turned back into the paddock where they immediately lay down and rolled, four black legs and four deep chestnut ones waving comically in the air as if they were trying out synchronized swimming without the water. There was no one in the house; everyone, including Drummer and Sidney, was still out in the grounds somewhere. We grabbed a cold drink and a packet of biscuits and went into the living room to wait for Roger's return. Soon we heard a car draw up and looked out to see Roger paying a taxi driver, reaching clumsily in his pocket with his left hand.

"Come on." Jonah legged it back to the kitchen with me following. We got there just as Roger walked in.

"Hello, Roger," Jonah said, trying to make his voice normal. "Had a good morning?"

"Fine thanks." There was a suspicious, upward flicker of his puckered lip. "You?"

"Very nice, though probably not as interesting as yours. We didn't have house plans and a deal to discuss, did we?"

The color drained immediately from Roger's face, making the scar stand out lividly.

"What the hell d'you mean?"

"We saw you in the pub," I said, adding less accurately, "And heard you."

"You pair of #@$%&." He snarled a very, very rude word. "You've both been a pain right from the start. Get off my back, will you?"

"Your voice is different." I stared at him. "Completely different."

"Shut up or I'll—" He raised his right fist threateningly and Jonah immediately stepped in front of me.

"And your injured hand appears to have mended miraculously too. Hurt Ellie and I'll break it again."

"Jonah!" Tom's face was a picture of horror as he clumped into the kitchen in his muddy wellies. "What did you say?"

"We've caught him out at last." I pointed eagerly at the scar-faced man. "And he just threatened to hit me!"

"Roger, is this true?" Tom turned toward him and my heart thumped into my socks as I realized he'd only heard what Jonah had said and not the real voice of the man pretending to be Roger.

"Of course not, Tom. I'm upset, I admit, and beginning to run out of patience with all the terrible things these two keep accusing me of." The hesitant, familiar quality was back, and I knew he was going to get away with it again.

"What's going on?" Sue appeared at the door.

"Jonah and Ellie have made another attack on me. I

haven't liked to tell you, but they're getting progressively crueler. Now, today, Jonah threatened to break my arm— you heard him, Tom, didn't you?"

Sue turned a stricken face to her husband. He nodded reluctantly.

"Only because he raised his fist to Ellie," Jonah cried out. "His right fist. We both saw him."

"And he used his real voice," I put in, without much hope they'd believe me.

"Real voice?" Sue sounded dazed. "What does Ellie mean, Roger?"

He shrugged dramatically, his right hand once more held awkwardly against his side. "She's lying. They're both lying, trying to convince you I'm not the real Roger Purley."

"Why would they lie?" It was the first time I'd seen Sue hesitate. I realized thankfully that she just wouldn't believe her son would threaten to use his fists then make up a story about it.

"Because it's the only way Jonah can stop you and Tom from doing the right thing and honoring my uncle's wishes. He knows he can't persuade you to take Garland House away from me so I'm afraid he's resorting to underhand methods. They've threatened violence on me before—ask Ricky, he saw Ellie deliberately ride her horse into me, I can even show you the bruises."

"Is that true?" Tom turned on Jonah.

"No! Oh, he might have marks on him, but he fell deliberately. Aslan didn't touch him."

There was a long silence while Sue and Tom stared at us both. I could hear how bad Roger had made it sound and didn't really blame them for being horrified.

Jonah plunged in, frantic to make his parents believe us. "We followed him today, Dad, into the pub at Ashey. He had the house plans with him, he's making some kind of deal about Garland with the guy he met there."

"A deal?" Tom was struggling to understand. "What kind of deal?"

"I don't know," Jonah admitted. "But he does."

All four of us looked at Roger and as soon as I saw the gleam in his puckered, twisted eye I knew he'd beaten us again.

He smiled ruefully and gestured with his left hand. "A

surprise. I wanted it to be a surprise for you both, that's why we met up in a pub and, of course, why I took Garland House's plans with me."

Tom and Sue watched him steadily.

"Martin's a specialist in country house interiors. I asked him to draw something up for the old west wing. He's to start work on refurbishing the bedrooms, at my expense of course, so you can have residential guests to learn about ecology and all the organic matters you're such experts in."

Sue gave a soft gasp and looked up at her husband.

"That's very generous of you Roger," Tom said gruffly.

"Generous my eye," Jonah said, only he didn't say eye. "If you weren't giving the house up you'd be able to use Silas's money to do it up yourself. Because of him you have to buy somewhere to live so don't start being grateful—"

"Jonah!" Tom's usually gentle voice was like thunder. "That's enough. Roger has explained himself fully. You've gone too far and you're grounded as from now. No friends in, no trips out."

"No friends!" Jonah swallowed angrily. "But Ellie—"

"Ellie seems to have behaved almost as badly as you and

is no longer welcome here."

I felt my lower lip tremble and struggled hard not to cry. Jonah took my hand and started walking, leaving the three of them there in the kitchen.

"Once Ellie has gone you go straight to your room." Tom still sounded completely unlike his usual kindly self.

By the time we got outside the tears had won their battle and were sliding slowly down my face.

"Don't cry," Jonah said miserably, taking my hand. "I won't let them stop me seeing you."

"You have to." I squeezed his hand. "We're in enough trouble as it is. Maybe after a few days apart they'll let me come back. I really like your parents and I can't bear them being mad at me."

"It's me they're wild at because they believe Roger that I'm a liar and a bully." He sounded deeply resentful. "We should have thought it through, got proof he was plotting something. Now he's got my mum and dad turned completely against us."

"You can't blame them for thinking he's telling the truth. He was totally convincing." I brushed away the tears, wishing hard we'd done as Jonah said and provided the Bartons with proper evidence. "I'll take Aslan back to Critchell Farm and maybe see you in a day or so?"

"Can I phone you?" He looked really upset at losing me, and if I wasn't feeling so bad I'd have felt good.

"Of course. Talk to you later." I broke free from him and went off to get Aslan from the field without looking back.

Drummer and Sidney were mooching around at the gate, and when I stooped to pat them good-bye they both wagged their tails and licked my hand so I started crying again. In fact I blubbered on and off practically the whole way back to the farm and was still red-eyed and miserable when Tara arrived an hour or so later.

"Whew!" She plonked herself down on the bed and stared at me. "What's going on? Sue said Tom has grounded Jonah and banned you. Why, what did you do?"

I told her the story, my voice flat and expressionless because I was all cried out.

"And you really thought Roger spoke in a different voice and used his right hand?" Even my best friend didn't believe me, I thought dully, so I suppose it was no surprise the

Bartons hadn't.

"Yes," was all I said.

She put her arm round me. "Look, I'm not being funny, El, but don't you think you might be imagining all this? I know how badly you want Roger to be a fake. Couldn't it just be wishful thinking on your part?"

"No!" I said more strongly. "Jonah heard and saw him too!"

She sighed and gave me another hug. "I'd like to back you up, honestly, but I've been watching him like anything and he's not slipped up once. Always uses his left hand, always speaks with that soft kind of stutter."

"That's because he's clever, not because he's real." I was fed up and wanted to do something. "I don't suppose you found out the name of his school?"

"Ooh yes, Ricky asked Sue and he wrote down what she said. Here you are."

She handed me a scrap of paper with FABERLY SCHOOL FOR BOYS and an address way up north written on it.

"It's a long shot but worth a try." I looked at her. "Would Duncan let me use his computer, do you think, or is he mad at me too?"

"He and Mary don't know anything. Sue and Tom aren't the kind to ring up and moan about you, are they?"

"No," I agreed, feeling sad I'd fallen out with such lovely people. "Will you ask Duncan if I can look something up on the Internet, then?"

She whizzed off straight away and soon I was typing FABERLY SCHOOL FOR BOYS in the search box on the Web. The hunt took a while but what do you know—another massive disappointment.

"What's up now?" Tara said, looking at my no doubt miserable face.

"I've drawn a complete blank. I was hoping to get names of anyone who was at school around the same time as Roger."

"Oh right. Don't the records go back that far then?"

"They don't go back at all. I can't find any mention of the school at all and I tried loads of websites, including that one where old pupils try to reunite with each other."

She gave a long, low whistle. "That's weird. It's definitely the school name Sue gave us."

"Yeah, thanks for getting it. It was a good idea but Roger wins yet again."

"I'm sorry, Ellie, really I am. I promise I'll keep trying to catch him out while we're searching."

"Thanks." I didn't hold out much hope; Roger was too much on his guard now. "Still ferreting around for the so-called missing will then?"

"Oh yes. He spends at least an hour every day and is going to start on the attics next week."

It sounded as though Roger was going to a lot of effort to convince the Bartons he really was trying to find this nonexistent will, and again I felt very, very depressed at the sheer efficiency of the man. The depression wasn't helped by the enforced separation from Jonah. True to his word he phoned every day, several times a day in fact, and although it was great talking to him we were both very aware that time was running out. Jonah wasn't at all surprised at the bad news about Roger's school.

"I knew it would be something like that. I'm not allowed near him of course, presumably in case I try to thump him, so I've no chance to catch him out. Rick said he'd keep trying, but the trouble is he still thinks the bloke is totally genuine."

"I know, Tara's the same, says we've talked ourselves into believing he fakes his hand injury and copies Roger's voice. Your mum remembers the way he spoke and that sideways tilt of his head that he does all the time. Whoever Roger really is, he's done his homework, and he's so good he's convinced everybody."

"Except us and we can't prove a thing." Jonah sounded as fed up as me. "And to make it worse I've still got another three days of being grounded."

Time was dragging for me too. Of course I still rode my darling Aslan every day and even had a go at setting up a jumping course in the corner of one of the fields. It just wasn't the same without Jonah, though, so when Mary suggested Tara and I go with her on a shopping trip to the nearby town of Lytchett, I agreed. Shopping isn't usually my idea of fun but it was better than moping around the farm. Duncan drove us, and he and Mary didn't mention Garland House or Jonah at all. Tara told me her godparents thought Jonah and I had quarreled and they were being tactful by not asking about it. It suited me; I really didn't want to have to go through the whole Roger Purley story with them. We had lunch in a nice restaurant, gorgeous tiger prawns and a pudding that had more chocolate than I'd ever tasted in one go.

Afterward we went for a wander round the town, which was one of those old-fashioned ones with lots of funny little shops tucked away in quiet corners. Mary wanted to try on a dress she saw in one of the windows, so while she and Duncan went in, Tara and I pottered around this little square, looking idly in all the other shops. One was an antiques place with a couple of pieces of beautiful old furniture and a silver tray bearing small trinkets. I don't know what made me look closer but I did—and completely froze. There, on the tray next to an elaborately decorated bowl, was a small, silver box. The lid was embossed with a coat of arms and I was sure, absolutely sure, I'd seen it before. In the library at Garland House was a circular oak table with a heavy glass top. Under the glass several items had been arranged: delicately colored feathers, a collection of tiny, pretty beads, some shells, and a small, silver box.

Chapter Twelve

I stared and stared at the box in the window, trying desperately to bring a clear picture of the one from the library into my mind. I was certain it was the same size and surely, surely that coat of arms was identical. There was a price ticket on the one I was staring at and I did a silent whistle at the amount they were asking.

"What's the matter? You look like you've seen a ghost." Tara was messily slurping on an ice cream.

"Look." I pointed. "That little box. Haven't you seen it before?"

"I've looked at a load like it, those snuffboxes I told you about in Silas's study. To be honest they all look the same to me."

I sighed in frustration and peered again, still sure the box was strikingly familiar. Tara, with her melting ice cream, couldn't come with me but I stepped boldly into the shop, making an old-fashioned bell clang noisily.

"May I help?" He was quite old and grumpy looking.

"The snuffbox in the window." I pointed. "Is it an unusual one?"

"Ah yes, yes, most rare, which of course is reflected in its price. It will be very, very sought after. I don't expect to keep it more than a few days."

"Really? You got it quite recently then?" I thought I was being very subtle, but he frowned at that.

"During the last week, yes. Why do you ask, is there a problem?"

There was no subtle way to carry on so I abandoned caution. "Did a man called Roger Purley sell it to you?"

He got very sniffy. "I don't have to answer that but no, that was not his name."

"Long scar down his face, right from above his eye to his chin, talks with—"

"I'm sorry, miss." He walked to the door and opened it pointedly. "If you have an objection to my selling this item you must get your parents to deal with it. I do not have public arguments with schoolchildren."

There was nothing to do but leave but I fumed silently, partly at being called a schoolchild if I'm honest. Still, I'm nothing if not persistent. If the snuffbox was from Garland's library there would be a gap in the table display that Tom and Sue would have to investigate. The shop owner would talk to them all right, I reasoned as I brought out my mobile phone to call Jonah.

"Hey." He sounded pleased to hear me but listened attentively while I told him what I'd seen.

"I'll check now and call you back."

I pictured him running swiftly, with his easy, long-legged style, into the old wing of the house. He didn't take long, but it wasn't the news I wanted.

"It's still there. At least, there's a silver snuffbox still in the table, but I'm not sure if it's the same one as before."

Not for the first time I cursed Roger's efficiency.

"He's put another one in its place, one of those he found in the study. The one he sold to the antiques dealer is rare and valuable, so Roger must have swapped it for an ordinary one."

"I'll tell Mum and Dad—" Jonah started.

I jumped in straightaway. "No, it's another thing we can't prove and they'll just get mad at us again. I don't want you grounded a second time."

"Nor me." He sounded very despondent. "At least I'll be able to see you on the weekend, but I'm just about giving up hope of sorting Roger. I got Ricky to ask him about Faberly School but the bloke just raised his eyebrows and said, 'How strange you couldn't find it. I must invite some of my old school chums round to tell you all about it.'"

"Oh great," I said. "He could get anyone to come along and pretend they used to know him."

"He doesn't have to bother." Jonah was very, very low. "Garland House will belong to him soon and it'll be too late for us to prove anything."

Again the days dragged slowly, and without Aslan I don't know how I'd have got through them. We were due to meet Jonah and Pharaoh on their first trip out since his punishment and I was really excited at the thought. Aslan, as usual, picked up my mood, prancing and cavorting enthusiastically as we set off for the moors. Jonah was already there, silhouetted against the sky, and my heart gave a very peculiar trampoline-type leap as he came galloping eagerly toward me. We talked nonstop, and even if it was mostly about Roger it was good to be sharing things in person rather than the previous week's phone calls.

"You know I told you about Ricky checking out the snuffbox in the library?" He was riding so close to me, our legs kept touching. "As you know he couldn't swear it was the same one but that's not surprising as we probably haven't ever looked at it really closely. Anyway, this morning he said it must be the same one because why would Roger pinch it when he's got all that money?"

"What money?" I said irritably.

"That's just what I said. Rick says Roger's spending like mad, including flowers for Mum and wine for Dad."

"Is your brother stupid?" I demanded unfairly. "If the bloke is nicking stuff from Garland and selling it he's bound to have a bit of cash."

"I know, I know, but Rick doesn't believe it, thinks it's all in our imagination——the voice and the right hand, all that. He's like Mum and Dad, believes Roger is Roger who has loads of money and is going to spend it all doing Garland up because he loves it so. It drives me mad none of them will believe us."

"We can't blame them really—Roger is completely convincing."

"But we know he's a phony—"

I shook my head wearily. "It's no good saying it, we've got to prove it."

"We're just going over and over the same old stuff, aren't we? Come on, we'll take the horses back and do some schooling. You and Aslan have a week's lessons to catch up and it'll give us something else to think about."

"But your mum and dad don't want me at Garland." I heard the tremble in my voice.

"Don't be soft." He pretended to be stern. "Come on."

I wasn't sure about going back with him but he was right: Once we started the jumping lesson I was too busy to worry about it. We started off back to basics with a few small jumps laid out in a serpentine shape.

"Everything in trot first," Jonah ordered. "The slower the pace, the greater the control."

He was right again, Aslan remained unhurried and in balance and I could feel he had time to use himself correctly. A trot stride is less than half the length of one at canter, so he found it easy to arrive "right" for the takeoff zone. Jonah emphasized the importance of a good approach by making an even, rounded turn into each obstacle. I knew squared or pointed turns would unbalance Aslan and make him lose rhythm and impulsion. Soon we had progressed to canter and Jonah taught me how I could help my pony by regulating the length of his stride on the approach. Any adjustments had to be made at least three strides before takeoff so that I was sure not to disturb and fiddle with him on those last important strides. It all went beautifully, and I was quite disappointed when Jonah called a halt.

"Tell him he's wonderful and put him in the stable for a rest," he said. "I'm not schooling Pharaoh today, I did loads with him last week when I couldn't go out."

"I should go." I felt nervous about seeing Tom and Sue.

"Nah. Come and have a drink. Mum and Dad are busy all day resiting a greenhouse. I've got to help later, so keep me company till then."

After settling Aslan, we walked over to the house, going in the back door as usual.

"Roger's not in, is he?" I asked quietly as we kicked off our boots.

"No, he went off somewhere this morning. Otherwise I wouldn't be coming in."

We made a sandwich and a drink and sat at the table in the bright, homey kitchen, trying hard not to talk about Roger, as it always seemed to get us in trouble. Tara came clattering in a bit later looking dirty and irritable.

"We're having hell of a job with the greenhouse," she said. "Can you go over and give a hand Jonah, I'm not being much help."

"Sure." He got up straightaway. "Not that I see the point. Roger Purley's going to change everything and—"

"Oh don't start!" Tara snapped. He shrugged and went out.

Once she'd washed her hands and face and had a long, cool drink she cheered up.

"There's no reason for me to go back now that Jonah's helping. I want to go into the nature reserve and see if I can spot a woodpecker Ricky saw this morning. I think it's a common sort we've seen loads of times but he reckons it's a lesser spotted."

D'you know I'd had no idea till this holiday just how keen my friend was on nature and stuff? I tried to look interested and probably failed dismally but she asked me to go along with her anyway. To be honest I'd rather have gone with Jonah and heaved bits of greenhouse around but I was still nervous about the reception I'd get from Sue and Tom so I agreed and we set off. Tara, who had her bird-watching binoculars slung round her neck, chatted away about the differences between types of woodpeckers; by the time we got to the nature reserve I was already bored. The tract of wild garden was quiet and serene, its lush foliage seeming to sleep in the warm sun.

"This way," Tara said quietly. I followed her noiselessly along a faint track that wound and twisted through the trees.

It was very beautiful in an untamed sort of way, and I began to understand the fascination it held for Tara. The only sounds were of birdsong, musical notes interspersed with cheeps and whistles, a soft breeze rustling the leaves above us, and, somewhere to our right, the gentle murmuring of flowing water. Although we were very near the house now it felt as though we were miles from anywhere, wandering through this oasis of natural beauty.

"Shh." Tara stopped suddenly. I nearly cannoned into her.

"What?" I hissed back.

She lifted the binoculars and started looking upward into the trees, searching every branch. I realized she must have caught sight of the elusive woodpecker and waited patiently for what seemed ages.

"I thought I saw—oh!" Tara, ace bird detective, moved swiftly onward and I followed.

Three times we did that. By now we'd curved a route directly toward Garland House and were standing only a few meters from the tall, narrow windows of the library. The ground between us and the house was a riotous tangle of undergrowth, looking quite impenetrable and unfriendly. Tara stood with her back to it and trained her binoculars on the trees we'd just come through. I was bored

again. I quite liked the quiet and calm and the whole idea
of this piece of natural wilderness, but spying on camera-
shy woodpeckers just wasn't my idea of a good time. Idly,
I looked across at the library windows—and did a double
take. There in the book-lined room were two figures. One
with his odd, hunched stance was clearly Roger, and with
him, I was sure, was the man in black, the one Jonah and
I had seen at the pub!

"Tara," I said and tapped her urgently on the shoulder.
"Lend me those glasses!"

"Gerrof!" She tried to twist away but I was quicker and
made a successful grab for the binoculars.

"Ellie!" she kind of shouted in a whisper as I spun back
and peered at the house through the powerful binoculars.

"I was right." I could see both men clearly, deep in conversation as they looked down at something on the table.

"What d'you mean you were right? I just caught my first
real glimpse of the woodpecker and now you've frightened
him off." She was shouting properly now.

"Sorry." I still wouldn't let her have the glasses. "It's
Roger and the man from the pub. They're in the library

and they're up to something."

"In the—" She made a sudden lunge and grabbed at the leather strap of the binoculars. "You mean you actually ruined my sighting because you saw Roger in his own house?"

"It's not his house." I tried to look through the glasses again. "And what's that bloke doing with him?"

"Tom and Sue know all about it. He's Martin and he's the interior designer, you thick head. He and Roger are planning the refurbishment."

"If you believe that you're stupider than you look." I gave a mighty heave and yanked the strap away from her.

"Me stupid! That's great coming from someone so dopey she has to pretend she sees Roger using his injured hand and talking in his own voice. It's pathetic the way you agree with everything Jonah says."

"What!" I was so outraged I could have thumped her. "I did see him use his hand and I did hear his real voice. You can't possibly believe I made it up just so Jonah would like me!"

"Can't I? You're nuts about him. I've never seen you like

it before and I reckon you'd back him up if he said the sky was pink with yellow spots. It's—it's pathetic!"

"So you said." I felt sick with anger. "So here's something else you won't like me doing either."

I held the binoculars by their strap and twirled them round my head.

"Ellie, don't—"

But it was too late, the glasses flew in a wide arc above our heads to land with a soft thud and rustle in the tangle of bramble and bracken between the house and us. Tara squealed and tried pushing her way through the greenery. Thorns tore at her clothes and hands and she stopped, then backed unhappily out again.

"You—you—"

To my dismay there were tears in her eyes. Although I was still mad at her I was sorry I'd dumped her precious binoculars in the undergrowth.

"I'll get them back." I started looking for a gap in the prickles but she didn't wait.

With a last, very un-Tara-like sob, she took to her heels and ran off, back along the track we'd come in by. I felt terrible, the sudden rush of anger having subsided, and I wished I hadn't reacted so violently. If I was honest, I couldn't blame her for not believing a word I'd said about Roger—as far as she and the Bartons were concerned it was all unsubstantiated rubbish. The one thing I must do was get her glasses back so at least I'd stand a chance of her continuing to be my friend. I poked around tentatively at the undergrowth, but it was clear that without a suit of armor I wasn't going to get through.

'A suit of armor—or a pony!' I thought and legged it swiftly back to the stable yard. Aslan was quietly dreaming in his box but glad to see me and we made our way quickly to the nature reserve and the track Tara and I had taken. I rode very quietly, keeping Aslan's pace slow and measured so we didn't frighten the wildlife too much. Back at the brambles I looked across the wide expanse of undergrowth to see if Roger and his "designer friend" Martin were still in the library. Without the binoculars I couldn't see their faces but could just make out their shapes, seated now at a table. Their heads were bent in concentration and I was glad to see they seemed far too engrossed to wander over to the window and look out.

I'd brought what I hoped were some useful things from the yard: a thick stable rug, a length of strong rope, a knife, and, as an afterthought, a sturdy torch I'd noticed in the tack room. If Aslan and I were going to hack our way through the undergrowth we needed all the help we could get, and a light, I figured, would probably be essential when searching among all that dense vegetation. I wrapped the rug around my pony's chest and urged him forward, leaning over his shoulder to chop away the long, thorny strands of the bramble. Aslan was wonderful, pushing strongly ahead and snapping the woody stems to make a pathway through the tangled mass. Every so often I switched on the torch, shining it downward in an effort to find Tara's binoculars. I just had to hope we were heading in the right direction and kept on pushing slowly forward. At last the strong beam of torchlight picked up a flash of something that glinted and I jumped off my pony's back to investigate.

The prickly brambles had thinned and now I was hunting through coarse clumps of grass and clinging ivy that grew vigorously over something buried in the ground. My groping fingers touched something solid. The binoculars! I grabbed at them, pulling great handfuls of ivy out of the way, tearing them up quite easily by their millions of shallow roots. I could see the glasses now and reached down eagerly, stopping in surprise as the light of my torch picked up the faded, rotting timbers of a gate or door that was providing the shallow foothold for the mass of ivy. I picked the binoculars up first, stowing them carefully in my jacket pocket, then bent again to clear more vegetation away. Gradually I exposed a door, a small, thick oblong of ancient wood with a rusting, ring-shaped handle. Breathing hard I stood up, braced my knees, and pulled the handle. Nothing happened except about two billion wood lice and centipedey things that I'd hoicked out of their ivy homes scuttled about madly. I threaded the rope end through the ring and yanked again with all my strength. This time the door gave a kind of squeaking groan, but still it wouldn't budge. Frustrated, I hacked back more of the undergrowth and tried once more. There was another creak and Aslan pushed me firmly in the back with his nose.

"What—oh Aslan, you clever boy, of course!" I realized at once what he was trying to tell me.

Keeping the rope threaded through the iron handle I tied the ends round his saddle, backing my pony carefully until I felt him take the strain. With a final, splintering creak the old door opened, crashing to the side in a cloud of old dirt and rotten leaves. I jumped like anything, and Aslan gave a startled twitch too. I undid the rope from his saddle and moved forward cautiously to peer inside the cavity that now yawned before us. My pony followed, and it felt comforting having him close up beside me. I switched the torch back on and shone it into a dark, dank-smelling tunnel stretching underground toward the walls of Garland House. It wasn't very high, but it was taller than me or Aslan, and I had to find out where it came out, didn't I? With my pony still keeping me very close company, I walked tremulously inside. The walls were of rough stone, filthy with damp and age, and apart from the torch and the rectangle of light from the open doorway there was no light, none at all. I hadn't realized quite how dense and black complete darkness is and I was very, very glad of the sturdy lamp and my beloved pony. We moved forward cautiously, shining the light along the dirty, cobweb-encrusted tunnel until, a short way ahead, I saw a pale glimmer of light. There was no sound, only our breathing and soft foot- and hoof falls on the spongy earth floor. Aslan's nose was level with my shoulder; I slipped my hand through his mane, interlocking the fingers, because it made me feel braver somehow.

The light ahead, when we reached it, was disappointing, coming from a grid in the stone ceiling that let in sweeter-smelling air and the faint glimmer I'd noticed. We moved on, having covered fifteen or twenty meters of gradually rising ground by now—and then I stopped, so suddenly Aslan nudged me again. Just ahead was another door, not as rickety looking as the first but very old and with the same kind of hoop-shaped handle. We went to it and I twisted the ring hopefully. To my surprise it turned fairly easily. I cautiously pushed the door open. I shone the torch, immediately seeing that the room was tiny, but before I had time to take the picture in I heard voices, quite clearly and obviously coming from somewhere behind the wall I was now staring at.

"So that's it—you're satisfied with the setup?" It was Roger, and I could hear the excitement in his voice.

"Oh yes. There will be formalities because of the age of the place but the size of the grounds makes any problems worth dealing with. As a development site, it's first class."

"So when do we sign?" Roger was so eager he was forgetting to stutter.

"As soon as you become the legal owner of Garland House. Your uncle's estate is due to be wound up in the next few days, you said?"

"Yes, absolutely. I'll go and chase up the lawyers now. The sooner I can sell, the better."

I was standing completely still, my fingers again entwined in Aslan's mane, clutching so tightly the hair was cutting into my skin. Jonah was right: The man calling himself Roger Purley had no love for Garland, had no plans to allow the Bartons to run their organic business from its grounds, had, in fact, every intention of selling it straightaway to some kind of property developer!

Chapter Thirteen

I stood there in the doorway of the tiny room and heard the scraping of chairs as Roger and Martin finished their discussion. I'd seen them sitting at a table so it didn't take a genius to work out that the tunnel Aslan and I had traveled led from the nature reserve to somewhere behind the bookshelves in the library. I listened for a few moments, barely daring to breathe, and put my hand softly over my pony's nose, my signal for him to keep still. I could hear nothing more and knew the two men must have left the room. Swiftly I shone the torch around the small space. There were cobwebs here too, festoons of them, looking dusty and creepy in the lamplight. I remembered reading about things called priest holes, built into old houses so that holy men could hide from religious persecution, but this small space had been used by someone more recent than a hundreds-of-years-ago priest.

It had once been a hideaway for a boy, a boy who'd brought in a stool, some adventure comics, and a rectangular box. There were candy wrappers on the dusty floor. It was easy to picture him sitting here, hidden from the world as he read or looked at the things stowed carefully in the box. I blew away the thick layer of dust from its top and opened it. The first thing I saw was a photo in a tarnished silver frame. I lifted it out carefully and looked at the bride and groom smiling out from the picture. Going by the style of their hair and clothes, I thought the wedding must have been around forty years ago, and my pulse quickened at the thought. Beneath the photo were some handwritten letters, not folded into envelopes but pressed flat, each one beginning "Dear Roger" and signed "your loving Mummy and Daddy." It wasn't until I exhaled in a great long sigh that I realized I'd been holding my breath. The boy who'd used this little hideaway leading into a secret passage had been Roger Purley.

There were more touching mementos of his parents: a mirror in a pretty, feminine frame, a briar pipe that still

smelled faintly of tobacco, and ticket stubs from long-ago
visits to a zoo, some cinemas, and train rides. I felt my eyes
begin to prickle at the thought of Roger, age fourteen like
me, hiding away to look at his memories of happier times
spent with his parents. At the bottom of the box, under-
neath a bathtime toy duck in faded yellow rubber, lay a
small photograph album, and I felt my fingers tremble
when I picked it up. The first picture showed the woman
from the wedding photo, smiling proudly down at a baby
wrapped in a white knitted shawl. There were several snap-
shots of her with a sturdy-looking toddler, and one of the
little boy sitting astride his daddy's shoulders. They were
so innocent and touching and I started to feel really emotional. It's hard to explain but even though I'd known the
man pretending to be Roger wasn't really Roger, my mind
had become somehow clouded and I hadn't imagined the
life of the real boy who'd lost his parents when he was only
my age.

Now, looking at the faded memories of the time he'd
spent with them, I felt a great surge of compassion and pity
for the Roger Purley I'd never met. There were school pho-

tos now, and I scrutinized the round, ordinary face that looked back at me. I was hoping of course that I'd be able to take this album to Sue and Tom and say, *Look, this is the real Roger, and he's nothing like the creep who's trying to trick you out of your house.* Unfortunately the photos showed no distinctive features or distinguishing marks, so they didn't prove anything at all. The slant of the head was very apparent—almost every shot showed Roger tilting his neck to one side—but the impostor did that all the time too. I replaced the album and absently picked up the rubber duck and the pretty mirror. It was surreal, standing in that tiny, cobwebby space that no one except Aslan and I knew about. My pony was standing patiently in the doorway, there being no room for him to join me, and I could see his reflection in the mirror. I held up the toy duck to show him and, trying to dispel the weird, spooky feeling of sadness, did his favorite impression.

"Look Aslan—qua-a-ck!"

He blew down his nose softly and tipped his fine head inquiringly.

I started to smile then said, "Why are you nodding to

the left instead of the right like you always do?"

He snorted again and I wheeled round. "Oh sorry, Aslan, it's me being dopey—seeing your reflection made me think it was left when really—" I stopped dead. "But—" I plunged my hand in the box and brought out Roger's album again, flipping excitedly through the pages. "Come on!" I put everything back in the box and tucked it under my arm. "We've got to find the others!"

Aslan backed up obediently and I slipped back into the tunnel, shutting the old door carefully behind me. The return trip wasn't at all spooky; instead of taking every step slowly and a bit fearfully I fairly thundered along with my pony's head once again level with my shoulder. I didn't bother trying to close the outer door; the crash it had made when I opened it had practically made it disintegrate. I grabbed the rug again to cover Aslan against the thorny brambles, and within a few minutes we were back on the nature reserve's track. Once we rejoined the grounds I put Aslan into canter and we fairly flew the short distance back to the stable yard. Tara was there, grooming Podge, who was nodding peacefully in the warm sun.

"Tara!" I slid to the ground and held out the box. "You won't believe what I've found!"

She tossed her head and carried on brushing. "A nice pair of bird-watching binoculars by any chance?"

"Oh," I said guiltily. "Yeah, I've got those and I'm really, really sorry I chucked them. I went straight in to get them back, look."

I handed the glasses over and she took them sniffily, still not looking at me.

"It was because of going into the undergrowth to find them that I found the tunnel." The words were tumbling over themselves. "It's some kind of secret passage and it leads to the library, well not into the library but a kind of hiding place behind it, and I've got proof that Roger's not Roger and—"

"Oh Ellie!" She thumped the body brush down and glared at me. "You've got to stop this obsession of yours."

"It's not—well maybe it is, but it's true. When Roger, the real Roger Purley came here he found either the tunnel or a way in from the library and he made it his secret hideaway. He took in comics and sweets and kept little mementos of his childhood with his mum and dad."

At last her mouth dropped open. "You're kidding!"

"No, honestly." I described finding the door and the creepy passageway and the sad little room. "And the man in black isn't a designer—he's a property developer, and Roger's selling him Garland House and all the grounds!"

"You're sure you didn't imagine that bit?" She was so infuriatingly stubborn.

I kept my temper. "No, I promise you. Look at the photos and you'll see I've been telling the truth all along."

She took the album and leafed slowly through it. "They're of Roger when he was a boy."

"*No!*" I said strongly. "Look again. Look how the boy in the pictures tilts his head."

"He still does that. Sue remembered him doing it back then and—" She stopped suddenly.

"Go on," I said encouragingly. "There's a difference, isn't there?"

"The photos all show the boy slanting his head to the right," she said slowly. "But Roger—"

"Who isn't Roger at all—he tilts his to the left!" I finished triumphantly. "It's because he practiced in a mirror, I reckon, and it's the only mistake he's made but it's enough. I'll just show these to Sue and Tom—"

"I wouldn't." She looked up. "Okay, okay, I know these do make it look bad for Roger, but he's convinced them that you and Jonah are fabricating stuff against him. They'll need stronger proof than this."

"But you believe it, don't you?"

"Ye-ah," she said, still a bit reluctantly. "I mean, I know that if someone has a lifelong mannerism they're not suddenly going to change it and start slanting their head the other way. It just wouldn't happen."

"Well then," I said belligerently.

"It's no good getting mad. I'm only telling you it's still hard to believe, and Sue and Tom will need something more positive. What we want to do is trick Roger into revealing his true self."

"Brilliant," I said snarkily. "Like Jonah and I never thought of that!"

"Well you haven't had much success have you?" she demanded (quite reasonably in fact). "What we need is to bring someone to the house who knew Roger well when he was here. It might be a good impersonation old scarface is doing, but it wouldn't fool anyone who'd lived here too."

"What d'you think we've been trying to do all these weeks?" I was glad she was on my side at last, but she was driving me mad stating the obvious. "We've tried the village, no one there knew him well, we can't trace his school, and his uncle and the old gardener are dead. Are you suggesting we dig those two up or something?"

"Calm down," she said severely. "What about the cook?"

"Mrs. Babbage? She retired to the seaside but we don't know where."

"If you couldn't find her it's probably safe to say the fake Roger Purley couldn't either." Tara had slipped easily into her brainy, analytical persona. "The man has obviously done his research well, made sure there's no one around who could tell he's not the real thing."

"What about the name that Sue gave us—Faberly School for Boys?" The more thoughtful she got the less rational I became.

"Don't be a moron. He made it up. Sue didn't know the name until he told her."

I gulped; it was obvious now she'd said it but fake Roger had brushed aside our challenge of the name with his usual confidence. "So," I said, fairly quietly and humbly. "We have to find Mrs. Babbage, do we?"

"There's no time. You heard Roger say he was hurrying up the lawyers so he can sell straightaway. There's only one thing to do."

"What?" I was still blank.

"You'll have to be the cook." She looked at me critically. "Close your mouth; you look half-witted."

"I think I am. How do I turn into Mrs. Babbage? She must be nearly ninety by now."

She sighed and led Podge back into the cool interior of his stable. "Put Aslan in and I'll work something out."

I meekly did as I was told. Twenty minutes later Tara was rehearsing me in my new role as the elderly former cook of Garland House.

"Just speak in my aunty Jane's voice," she instructed. "Fake Roger never heard Mrs. Babbage talk, so any elderly-sounding woman will do. And you're brilliant at that."

I was glad I was getting some praise at last.

"I'll nip over to the Bartons and tell them they've got a visitor," she went on. "I'll put Ricky and Jonah in the picture first so they can help set up the trap."

"Do I have to dress up?" I was feeling nervous. It was one thing to muck around doing impressions for a laugh; this was different.

"You'd better. I'm hoping Roger will just listen at the door and not see you but maybe you'd better put a long cloaky thing on in case he bursts into the room."

I didn't fancy an enraged scar-faced man flying across the library at me so I went off to the attic to find a good disguise. There were loads of old clothes up there and boxes of ornaments and paintings that had obviously been rifled through very recently, presumably by Roger looking for salable items while pretending to be will hunting. Tara's plan was simple, but it all hinged on getting the timing right. I checked my watch worriedly as I pulled on a long, bulky dress and topped it with a heavy, hooded coat. Quite who would dress like this on a summer's day was beyond me but all I wanted was to not look like me and I succeeded pretty well at that. I checked the time again and hurried downstairs to the library. It was empty and silent but in my hyped-up state I felt as though someone was there watching me. I looked furtively at the book-lined walls, trying to work out exactly where the little hidey-hole was sited.

I wasn't feeling very confident about my hurried disguise so I drew the faded curtains until the room was shrouded in a dim, spooky light. The time dragged horribly slowly. I paced nervously up and down, my long skirt making a swooshing noise on the wood-block floor. Then, at last, the door opened and Tara hurried in. She must have been nervous too, or maybe she didn't expect to see a hooded, muffled figure prowling round in a murky half-light. She jumped anyway and let out a small, startled squeak but recovered quickly and went straight into our planned dialogue.

"Hello, Mrs. Babbage, how nice to meet you. Ricky has gone to fetch his parents, I'm not sure if you ever met them?"

I ran my tongue over dry lips, cleared my throat, and in Aunty Jane's rambling elderly voice said, "No, dear, I didn't, I left Garland House before they arrived. It's young Master Roger I've come to see—it will be such a treat because we were close, very close, you know."

"Really?" Tara's acting was dead good; I just hoped mine was as convincing. "You do know he's been in a car crash and is scarred quite badly?"

"Yes, yes, Jonah Barton told me when he rang but I said not to worry, I'd know Roger Purley anywhere, scars or not—"

The door burst open and a madman stood there, shaking his fist while the deep scar on his face turned an ugly, livid red.

"You little cow!" he snarled at Tara as I swept rapidly out of sight behind a high-backed chair.

"Who is this, dear?" My voice was genuinely trembly, making it sound even older. "Not Roger, I can see that."

"Interfering old—" He made a sudden plunge toward me. I tried to run, hampered by the long, heavy clothes. Roger's hands were outstretched, both of them itching to get "Mrs. Babbage" by the throat. "I'll shut you up the pair of you. I only need a few more hours and the house is mine."

For a truly dreadful moment I thought he was going to get me then, but suddenly, wonderfully, a section of the bookshelves swung forward and Jonah, tall, strong, and very angry, came running toward us. He grabbed Roger's left arm and twisted it savagely behind his back.

"You touch her and you're dead meat!"

Roger cursed and swung wild punches with his right fist, missing Jonah completely.

"How did you find the old hag?"

"We knew Mrs. Babbage was the only person who could identify the real Roger." Tara slipped back into brain box mode. "And she has just said you are definitely not him."

"The old bag! I can still win, I'll just tell the Bartons that the old Babbage woman is senile, can't possibly identify anybody correctly. They'll believe me, they always do."

"Not this time, Roger, or whatever your real name is." Tom, followed by Sue and Ricky, came quietly into the room. "We've heard enough to know Mrs. Babbage is telling the truth."

The scar-faced man collapsed like a burst balloon, slumping defeatedly into a chair. "I couldn't trace her, she was the only detail I didn't take care of. All the money I'd have got for this place gone just because a batty old woman knows I'm not the real Roger Purley."

"Well, now that you've admitted it at last I can take off this horrible coat." I whipped the thing off and shook out my hair.

Tom and Sue's faces were an absolute picture, and I thought fake Roger was going to have a heart attack. It was absolutely the best moment I'd ever enjoyed that didn't involve Aslan, particularly as Jonah was looking at me with utter pride and something I thought might be much more . . .

So, that's it really. The rest of our stay at Critchell Farm was brilliant and the Garland House Horse Show an absolute triumph. Aslan and I won the Novice Jumping while Jonah and Pharaoh just squeaked a victory in a jump-off against the clock in the Open class. Tara and Ricky gave the small kids pony rides on the ever-patient Podge and showed off the amazing knowledge they'd both gained by answering questions from the parents about Garland's organic gardening policies. We had to go home a couple of days afterward but Jonah and I still talk every day and I'm going back to Garland House at half term with Tara and her mum.

Oh, I suppose you want to know about all those loose ends we had to tie up? I must say the generosity and compassion shown by Tom and Sue continued to amaze me when they agreed not to report fake Roger to the police as long as he told them the whole truth. I knew Sue had fretted a great deal in case Silas's real nephew had been unfairly denied inheriting Garland House, so I was really, really glad for her when her mind was at last put to rest. Not only was the genuine Roger Purley dead without having left any family, but there had never been the slightest chance that Silas would have left the house to him.

The scar-faced man, whose real name was Aaron Blackwood, told us quite unrepentantly, "Roger and old man

Crawford didn't get on at all, practically hated each other, but I figured there'd be no one around who knew that so I played on the story that they'd been real close. It nearly worked too, I had most of you believing it, even got you hunting for a will Silas never made."

I could see Jonah was still itching to thump him but I have to confess I had a sneaking desire to laugh at Aaron and the outrageously cheeky pride he took in telling us how he'd decided to turn himself into Roger Purley. Roger had been his employer for some time and over the years had talked of his early life. He was a proper misery apparently, but he had something that out-of-work actor Aaron Blackwood didn't: money. Roger was still living off the substantial sum inherited from his parents and paid Aaron to be his driver, minder, organizer, whatever was needed. Always restless, Roger moved from state to state, providing Aaron with an easy lifestyle and no bills.

The move to California was the longest trip they'd ever made and the first time Roger had decided to share the driving of the rental truck they used. Aaron didn't even see the barrier the truck hit on the highway, didn't know anything about being dragged from the burning wreck till he woke up in hospital days later. He'd always been good at thinking on his feet, and although he was actually flat on his back with multiple injuries, he realized immediately that the best way forward was for him to become Roger Purley; the dead driver, whose body was so badly burned it was unrecognizable, would therefore be Aaron Blackwood.

"As well as money in the bank Roger had medical insurance and I didn't." He was completely matter-of-fact about it. "I was in hospital for months and because the staff accepted I was Roger Purley, the insurance company did too. They sent a guy to see me, obviously, but I was the right age and build, spoke with that stuttering English accent Roger had, and of course signed everything left-handed because of my injuries."

"But you can use your right arm." I looked at his hands with a bit of a shudder, remembering them stretched out to grab "Mrs. Babbage" round the throat.

"Sure I can, it was only a simple break, but I kept up the pretense so there wouldn't be any inquiries about the difference in Roger's signature—which I was using a lot."

"On things like checks and credit cards no doubt." Sue looked disgusted, and I wondered if I was the only one who found Aaron's sheer nerve amusing.

"You got it. The bank accepted I was Roger and I set up his new left-handed signature without too much bother."

"So, if you had all his money, why did you come over here and try to steal Garland House from us?" Jonah was definitely not finding him funny.

"I spent it all," Aaron said simply, his mouth lifting in the odd, puckered grin. "A couple of failed business ventures, bit of gambling, you know how it goes. So when I saw the ad asking for the whereabouts of Roger Purley I thought, *What the hell, let's go for it.* I knew the background and although there was no chance Silas would have left Roger anything I banked on no one knowing that. It was worth a try to con you lot out of a few quid. I gotta say I was blown away when you agreed I should get the actual house."

He said it so openly and with such frank amazement

I'm sure I wasn't the only one who wanted to laugh. Neither the Bartons nor Tara and I ever admitted actually admiring Aaron's sheer, mind-boggling effrontery, but I think we all wondered just what he'd get up to next. He told us his plan was to return to acting.

"I must be pretty good," he pointed out cheerfully. "Getting the accent right and all that. I think I'll try auditioning for horror films now I've got the face for it."

That made even Jonah's lips twitch, but he was adamant he'd never feel the least bit of kindness or pity for Aaron Blackwood.

"That cheeky-chappie routine was just another acting role. The guy is a complete creep and no one's to feel sorry for him. Look what he nearly cost us!"

"True," his brother said, watching the taxi taking Aaron out of our lives and no doubt into more trouble. "And I have to apologize for not believing you and Ellie sooner."

"Me too." Tara was in her favorite position, lolling lazily, this time flat out in the sweet-smelling grass of the paddock. "If we'd joined forces earlier and worked together we'd have got rid of old scarface a lot quicker."

"Mum and Dad feel bad they doubted you too, though they did try to contact Mrs. Babbage just in case she could prove you were right." Ricky grinned suddenly. "That's why they got such a shock when you took off that hood thing, Ellie. Up till then they thought you were the real thing."

"So did young Master Roger," I said in my Aunty Jane voice. "Such a good idea of yours, Tara. It gave him a terrible jolt finding out he wasn't the only actor in the place!"

"You were brilliant, Ellie." Jonah's dark eyes definitely had *the* look in them. "And finding the secret passage was amazing too. We had no idea there was such a thing in the library, and the fact that we turned that part of the grounds into a nature reserve meant the entrance outside would never have been found if it weren't for you."

"And my bad temper." I still felt bad about chucking those binoculars. "And I only got through the undergrowth because of Aslan."

Tara smiled lazily at me. "Yeah, and I only came up with the Mrs. Babbage idea because of your pony as well."

"How come?" Jonah and Ricky were puzzled.

Tara sat up and threw grass at them. "Because, you dopes, I didn't believe Roger wasn't Roger—not until Ellie showed me the photos and told me what she'd realized when she saw her horse in the mirror!"

JENNY HUGHES lives in Dorset, England. She has written twenty-two horse novels for young adults, which have been published in eight countries. Jenny's books are based on her experience working at a farm, at a riding school, and with polo ponies; but most of all they spring from her deep love of horses and the joy of sharing her life with such amazing beings.

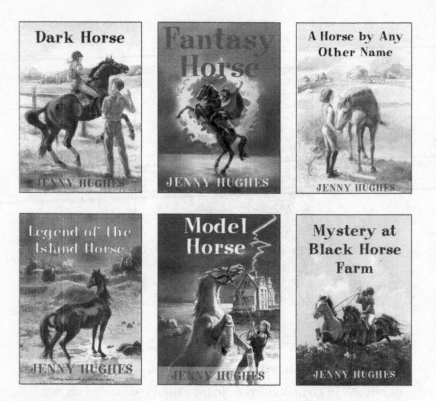